I KNOW YOU NOW

I KNOW YOU NOW

Sushant Changotra

PRABHAT
PAPERBACKS

Published by
PRABHAT PAPERBACKS
4/19 Asaf Ali Road,
New Delhi-110 002 (INDIA)
e-mail: prabhatbooks@gmail.com

ISBN 978-93-90378-08-1
I KNOW YOU NOW
Novel by Shri Sushant Changotra

Edition
First, 2020

Price
₹ 195.00 (Rupees One Hundred Ninty Five only)

Printed at
R-Tech Offset Printers, Delhi

This book is dedicated to my family, to all those people who have knowingly or unknowingly inspired me and to the entire cosmos for blessing me!

Preface

My sincere gratitude to you dear reader, for picking up this book and for giving me the joy of being read.

I feel that life is a vehicle for achieving the soul's destiny. There isn't a life, which has not seen its share of highs and lows. We all make our shares of mistakes, but some lives get squandered in the mazes of complicated situations. In testing times, we need a helping hand to see us through the rough patches. More often than not, stories become one's best guides and the imaginary characters in them end up as one's true friends.

I have always felt inspired to narrate the story, which fulfilled the aforesaid role and celebrated the joy of human relations and the importance of love, honesty and commitment in our lives.

This story has been a part of my life for over two years. It has given me immense joy to write it and it has truly been a surreal experience. Every chapter of this story has added so much perspective to my own thinking that indeed writing it has turned out to be the most enriching experience of my life.

Acknowledgments

If words could describe my gratitude to all the lovely people in my life, I would thank the words for it.

As a young boy, I made a promise to my late father Sh. Naresh Changotra that I would make him proud and I guess that promise continues to drive me further. I know Dad, that you continue to bless me from wherever you are. I cannot thank you enough for the role model you have been for me.

I am deeply indebted to my sweet mother, Mrs. Vijay Changotra. She does not cease to encourage this dark horse of the family in everything and anything that he does. She is my source of inspiration in so many ways.

The biggest motivator for putting this work on paper has been my soul mate Dr. Sakshi Sharma. She egged me to start writing when I myself did not know whether I could pen down my thoughts satisfactorily. She has been my prime motivator and an honest critique.

The penchant for new stories of my sweet daughters—Aadya and Miraya has kept the storyteller in me alive and kicking.

My sister Priti, who has always been the most patient listener to me and has been and will be one of my biggest supports. My brother Dr. Parshant, who introduced me to the world of stories in our childhood by reading comics to me even when I couldn't read them properly.

My heartfelt gratitude to Mr. Rohit Bhradwaj, Sh. Virender

Sharma, Smt. Suniti Sharma, Sera and Sh. Jatinder Pal for their unconditional love and for being there for me at all the times.

My sincere thanks to dear Akhil Dogra, Aashish Sharma, Dr. Alok Joshi, Arjun, Sh. Ashok Kumar and Late Sh. Surinder Mohan Ojha for being a source of motivation for me.

My heartfelt thanks to my pillars of strength—my friends—Gautam, Chanderjit, Rohit Mehra, Rohit Watts, Rishi, Rajat Joshi, Sachin, Sudhir, Ankit, Ashwini Dubey, Sandeep, Munish, Aman, Chanan, Jitender, Ankur, Manisha, Jassi, Vinni, Harvinder, Pardeep and Anubhav and special thanks to Sh. Medha Shri for editing and guiding.

Most of all, to the great institution of the judiciary: for giving me the opportunity to meet a diverse lot of people. I have been blessed to have learned senior colleagues like Smt. Poonam Bamba, Sh. N.S. Gill and Sh. Bharat Parashar who have always guided me in their own ways.

My deepest gratitude is reserved for the Almighty, who looks over all of us.

I express my gratitude as well as sincere apologies to all those friends, colleagues and relatives whose names couldn't find mention herein due to space constraints but my gratitude goes to each one of them, who have enriched my life.

Contents

Preface 7
Acknowledgment 9

Chapter - 1 13
Chapter - 2 19
Chapter - 3 23
Chapter - 4 26
Chapter - 5 31
Chapter - 6 40
Chapter - 7 47
Chapter - 8 53
Chapter - 9 57
Chapter - 10 65
Chapter - 11 76
Chapter - 12 81
Chapter - 13 89
Chapter - 14 101
Chapter - 15 112
Chapter - 16 121
Chapter - 17 130
Chapter - 18 140
Chapter - 19 147
Chapter - 20 155
Chapter - 21 161

Chapter - 1

The clock was already striking ten and Nitin was still locked up in his room with no sign of getting up anytime soon. Shantanu was getting late and Sushmita could sense the edginess in his tone. The results of JEE had been declared just a fortnight ago and Nitin's good result in the engineering competitive exam was the reason that had Shantanu's temper under the lid. On any normal day, Shantanu would have thundered prolific expletives on Nitin for sleeping so late; but now he was making special effort to keep himself calm.

At last his persistent effort failed and he blurted out to Sushmita in his deep voice, "Is Steve Jobs going to wake up or will he join the Delhi College of Engineering in his sleep only?" Sushmita tried to ignore the usual remarks coming out from the self-proclaimed monarch of their house. It rather irked Shantanu and as he was departing, having picked up his lunch box, he spoke again, "Don't spoil him so much that he fails to value the importance of discipline". The door closed with a thud and out went Shantanu. With the fading sound of the scooter Sushmita could make out the distance that agonizing persistent trauma had traveled with it.

Finally, the decibels of engine of Shantanu's scooter turned to nil. Although, with it the seemingly non-existent whirlpool of thoughts inside Sushmita's mind and heart should have subsided, however, it was not to be. Instead quietly the tears came rolling down her cheeks but still their warmth was not able to break the circle of thoughts which were gearing up inside her.

Lost in her thoughts, Sushmita was thinking out loudly to herself that what wrong had she done to deserve such a life of constant struggle and bashing at the hands of her husband, to who she had always remained so devoted. The more she thought about her miserable condition, more she was convinced that her destiny had brought all this misery upon her. Otherwise, there was no reason for all this bitterness from Shantanu, that too when Nitin had done so brilliantly well and had surpassed every expectation that Shantanu had from him and still he continued to rebuke them. She was sure that today's outburst was not directed towards Nitin, but was an assault on her. The boy had done exceedingly well, she felt that infact it was Shantanu's dissatisfaction towards her that came out in the form of such constant reprimands.

Outside, suddenly the clouds had started gathering, as if someone was listening to Sushmita's soul searching and was trying to match it.

Oblivious to the developments in his house, Nitin was fast asleep. The wind had picked up with the changing weather outside. The windowpane next to his head was constantly striking the wall, as if it was trying its best to pull him out of the deep slumber. On the contrary, the cool breeze was sweeping his calm face pushing him further into deep slumber and what could trouble a calm mind?

Nitin's new Samsung mobile phone was buzzing since early morning. The new phone was his prized possession for the last three days. It was a gift from his mother, who had kept her promise of buying him the phone of his choice upon being successful in competitive entrance exam. It had cost her all her savings, which she had done without Shantanu's knowledge. He loved his mother with all his heart and this gesture had further endeared him to her.

Nitin's result had brought rare joy to this small family of three. No doubt Nitin was on cloud nine. He was being hailed as a shining example of success in the neighborhood.

On the other hand, Sushmita was trying to keep her emotions under check and had begun her daily chores. She was dusting the house, wherein a speck of dust was hard to be found. While wiping the dining table, she was wondering that a week ago Shantanu had looked so pleased while accepting greetings from his family members and friends. He had even patted Nitin on his back when the news of Nitin's good ranking had broken. She always knew that he was a little hesitant in displaying his feelings; probably that is why he did not hug his only son even then.

Her thoughts drifted to eighteen years ago, when she came in this house after being married at the age of twenty. Shantanu was not the kind of man which every girl would dream of getting married to. He was five years older to her, had a small paunch, but was fairly taller with wheatish complexion and even then, had a moustache, whereas, she herself was a petite young girl. All her friends used to admire her black almond shaped eyes. They used to chide her that her eyes had captivating appeal and her mother was proud of her hair, which she would tightly braid.

For the first two months after their marriage, she had silently expected that Shantanu would praise her beautiful eyes or long hair. Every evening, she would get ready before Shantanu's arrival with a simmering hope that he would be startled by her beauty and would admire how lucky he was to have her as his wife. Once she saw that it was not coming forth, slowly and steadily she resigned to her fate and accepted that her husband was different from what her expectations were of him.

Every time she thought about Shantanu's coldness towards her unspoken feelings, it would set her heart aflame. The falling apart of her dreams sprouted in childhood, nourished in teenage and nurtured in the prime of her youth was difficult to accept. She would often sob and sometimes curse her fate because for her at that age, marriage was the only thing that occupied most of her thoughts. She kept these mental tribulations to herself and did not show any sign of frustration to Shantanu or to her relatives including her own mother.

Before getting married, she had often heard her mother crib that 'marriages are nothing but compromises'. She used to detest this phrase from the core of her heart. Every night before going to sleep she used to pray to God to bless her with life made beautiful by her family members. Gradually she accepted the things as they were and made a compromise with her life.

In a few months' time she gave the news to Shantanu about arrival of a beautiful life within her body, which was to be their first child. As expected Shantanu was pleased, but wasn't overjoyed. Happiness still seemed to elude him on the day when he could have been the happiest person on earth, but this did not prevent Sushmita from enjoying the bliss. She had got the reason to be happy and the reason to call someone truly her own. She had found her own source of happiness and eternal joy. Now she was happy to be herself and with the changing size of her body, the bounds her happiness also kept expanding. She would go hysterical upon feeling the kicks in her belly, used to talk to the unknown for hours and hours or would read *'Gita'* to it. The journey of these nine months turned her life from going towards deluge of darkness to the brightness of a beautiful clear sky. She was waiting for the day of arrival of someone whom she already loved in a deep and unconditional way.

The gynecologist had given her the due date of 9th October. As the last week approached, Shantanu called his cousin Sangeeta to stay with Sushmita while he was away to work. He had given clear directions to call him on the telephone of his office and had also written the phone numbers with sketch pen on the door of their bedroom. He had also made a request to their neighbor Mr. Bhatia to allow his sister to use their phone in case of emergency. He was making all the preparations, which a responsible father should have made. Sushmita on the other hand was oblivious to all of this. The face of Shantanu showed tension written on it, while Sushmita's face painted a picture of serenity.

On the morning of 6th October, Sushmita started feeling uneasy. Shantanu called the gynecologist and narrated the symptoms to her, but the doctor told him to wait. Unwillingly Shantanu went to his office that day a bit later than his normal timings. After about one hour her water burst and Sushmita started writhing in pain. Sangeeta felt panic-stricken, went numb and fainted.

Even in excruciating pain, Sushmita assessed the situation and analyzed that she had to be rushed to the hospital. With great difficulty she moved her large body to the door of their neighbor. Alas, a lock was hanging on the latch of the door. Perhaps Mrs. Bhatia, who used to be alone at that hour, had gone to the grocery shop. Determined not to panic, Sushmita slowly started moving towards market and she had hardly walked for 50 meters, when she saw Shantanu coming from ahead. Having seen her, Shantanu dashed towards her and firmly held her in his arms. A smile of relief, love, admiration and exhaustion passed through her face and she fainted.

It seemed that the child in her womb also loved her so deeply that he could not wait any longer to feel the touch of the hands, which would cradle him till they lasted. The wait was about to be over and the most beautiful bond on earth was about to begin. The reason of her life was coming.

□

Chapter - 2

Sushmita went to Nitin's room, but he was fast asleep. To her, Nitin was still her darling baby boy. She went back to kitchen and again got immersed in her thoughts.

The memories of those days were still fresh in her mind. Her thoughts wandered back to the room of the hospital. Upon hearing the beeps of instruments she opened her eyes and could see the doctor saying something to her, but could not make out what she was saying and passed out again.

After sometime, Sushmita again opened her eyes slowly and heard the crying sound of baby. She saw the nurse standing beside her bed, injecting medicines in her drip. She mustered all her strength and said, 'My baby?' The nurse turned and gave her an assuring smile and said, 'He is beautiful!' Their eyes met, Sushmita and the nurse exchanged smiles, and one pair of eyes amongst them turned moist. The nurse picked up the crying baby lying next to her in the cradle and brought him near Sushmita. She got up from the bed as if suddenly all the pain had vanished. She held her beautiful baby boy for the first time and took him in her embrace. The child also stopped crying, as if he identified his mother's warmth and touch. Silence prevailed in the room and the middle-aged nurse who had witnessed many such magical moments was absorbing it once again. The serenity in the cascade of emotions on display was touching her as well.

The silence was finally broken by the creaking sound of the door as the doctor arrived with her team. 'Congratulations Sushmita your son is as beautiful as you. Both of you gave us really tough time. Your condition was very critical when you were brought in. For now, you enjoy your motherhood, but we will have to discuss about few issues later on and don't keep your little one hungry now'. The doctor smiled and left after checking the reports.

After three days both the mother and son were discharged from the hospital, but not before Sushmita was told that she will not be able to give birth again. Sushmita had responded to the devastating news very calmly. Her display of courage had astounded the doctor as well. She had taken it with the pinch of salt.

On their arrival at home, they were greeted by smiling faces of people in the neighborhood. After performing customary traditions for the arrival of the newborn, Sangeeta profusely apologized from Sushmita about the whole fiasco. She moved around the house doing the necessary chores, trying to take care of mother-son duo. The vigor in her steps showed the repentance she had towards Sushmita. The same evening, Mrs. Bhatia came to congratulate the family. Mr. Bhatia apologized on bhalf of Mrs. Bhatia as she did not have inkling that such situation could have arisen. Shantanu readily accepted the apologies and courteously took the greetings.

For a month Sushmita and Sangeeta worked tirelessly taking shifts in nursing the baby. Their bond of friendship grew stronger by the day, largely because of mutual respect they shared. After about a month and half, Sangeeta left for her home promising Sushmita to return soon. Sushmita knew that she would miss Sangeeta not because she needed her help, but because she had become the second closest person to her.

Sushmita immersed herself completely into caring of her darling baby boy. To the outer eye her toiling would have appeared brutal, but she herself was at peace. For her caring and nurturing of her son was nothing less than spiritual devotion.

Lost in her thoughts, Sushmita did not realize that she was cleaning the slabs of the kitchen. The entire journey of growth of Nitin from a toddler to young boy flashed before her, how she had reacted when Nitin had started crawling, the moment when she had taken him to the school for the first time and many a times when Nitin had performed in school functions or was awarded prizes for excellence. She failed to remember how many times Shantanu had accompanied her on any such occasions. When Nitin had started growing up, she had even told Shantanu how he missed his presence, but every time she had met with a curt response that he had to win the bread for family and Nitin was able to study in good school because he was working hard. The train of her thoughts was derailed by the sound of doorbell. She shuddered a little as if someone had shaken her while she was asleep. In her disconcerted state of mind, she failed to register that her hand had accidentally hit the knob of the gas stove.

Quickly she went to the main door only to find a sales person trying to sell water purifier. As she walked past the living area, her gaze fell on the wall clock. It was 11.10 a.m. Realizing that it was late and she still had to cook breakfast and lunch, she thought of completing her daily ablutions first. With few quick steps, she reached the kitchen where she had a small '*Mandir*' in one of the cabinets. Hastily she picked up the matchbox and took out one matchstick for lighting a lamp. Then all hell broke loose!

Nitin woke up to heart piercing shrieks of his mother.

His heart skipped a beat when he saw his mother engulfed in flames. Still dazed for a moment he couldn't realize whether he was asleep or awake. The burning picture of his mother was something he could not grasp. Without realizing what he was doing, he picked up a blanket and jumped onto his mother who was frantically moving around. He latched on to her trying to douse the flames. The burning body of his mother was so hot, that as a reflex action, he moved away. He again saw that her '*salwar suit*' was still on fire. He picked up whatever his hands went up to and wrapped up his mother in his arms and this time, he did not let her go.

In no time there were many people running around in their house. Frantic calls were being made. Nitin was holding on to his mother who was not moving now. People were arguing and shouting at each other. Someone was saying they should put the heap of dry flour on her, others were saying that they should pour milk and someone was calling his brother to bring the car. In all this commotion, laid two humans figures quietly-the mother and son duo. One was incapable of saying anything and the other was unable to. In a span of five minutes their destiny had taken a sharp turn from blissfulness to utter misery.

Nitin was still holding on to his mother. He could feel her heartbeat. With all his might, he was praying to god for letting it continue its beating. Hope is such a powerful thread that it binds reality to imagination and he was clinging on to it ever so strongly.

Suddenly, he went pale and his own body limped. He could not feel her heart beat. His heart sank. He closed his eyes and kept praying to god that it was a dream and he would wake up to find his beautiful mother smiling at him again.

□

Chapter - 3

The visit to the hospital was a mere formality. The doctor Immediately declared Sushmita as brought dead. The doctors took Nitin to emergency ward to tend to burn injuries on both his arms and some parts of his chest and neck. Even after being treated, he remained seated on the bed of ward. His gaze stuck to a portion of wall in front. The numbness of his senses was so profound that his mind could not comprehend the catastrophe that had hit him. In this agonizing moment, loss did not make sense.

On receiving the news, Shantanu rushed to the hospital. Straight away he went to see the last mortal remains of his wife of eighteen years. On seeing her body in such charred condition, he started crying like a child, if not solely for his affections towards her, then also for the condition in which she breathed her last. After 10-15 minutes, when he was able to control himself, he was taken to Nitin. On seeing Nitin, Shantanu hugged him and started crying uncontrollably. His hugs got no response and his wails came back with an echo. Nitin was no more than a dead wood.

The dead body of Sushmita was brought to their home and it was laid to rest in the living area of their small house. Despite several entreaties, Nitin refused to move from his mother's side. With every moment the wailing of near and dear ones, friends and relatives grew louder and louder as

Sushmita was loved by one and all. The loud cries of relatives including Sangeeta would every now and then break the shackles of control of Shantanu, however, nothing propelled a tear from Nitin's eyes.

People tried to cover Sushmita's face with the shroud, but Nitin kept removing the cover. Nothing else mattered to him, as it never had, except for his love for his mother. The face of Sushmita had been charred beyond recognition, her nose had melted, the eyelids could hardly be seen and her long hair were gone and yet all Nitin could see was the beautiful face of his mother with her long sharp nose, her beautiful almond shaped eyes and her long black hair falling on her forehead. He could see her smiling towards him.

It was decided that the condition of Sushmita's body was not good; therefore, cremation should be done on the same day. It took them more than one hour to reach the crematorium, which was otherwise hardly at a distance of twenty minutes' drive. It seemed that the heavens were also crying their heart out on the untimely demise of a truly special human and it rained cats and dogs.

After the performance of rituals, everyone except close relatives left for their homes. Not only was Sushmita's untimely and tragic death, but Nitin's state of shock was also talk of the town. Now it had started disturbing Shantanu as well, because Nitin did not weep at the cremation as well. He took it upon himself to remain near Nitin. As they returned home, Nitin went to his room, closed his eyes and fell on the bed. Shantanu followed him, but thought that he will be exhausted and it will be better if he sleeps. He pulled the door and closed it. His idea turned out correct. The exhaustion took over and Nitin fell asleep.

At midnight, Nitin woke up. In a few moments he started

humming the song "*Chanda Hai Tu....*", he remembered that it was the song his mother used to teach him. She always thought that he was good at singing and she used to encourage him by singing along with him. He loved such singing sessions with her. One day, as both of them were singing together, Shantanu came home and lambasted Sushmita for wasting Nitin's energy and focus on such useless things instead of making him study. He blamed Sushmita for being shortsighted as education alone was necessary for their son's good future. Nitin had seen tears swell up in her eyes, but she did not say anything.

In this moment, it dawned upon Nitin that it was his mother only, who understood him. He realized, how much she loved him and how she cared for him. How he was left alone by her absence and how much he loved her. He let out a sigh and his feelings poured out as the words, 'I love you mom; please come back' escaped from his lips.

The clouds of emotions inside him were now ready to pour and it rained all night. Shantanu and Sangeeta came inside. Shantanu could not gather courage to say anything. Sangeeta who was next to his mother hugged him. Nitin also hugged her back and he shouted and cried, wept and again cried till the clouds had shed all the water they had. The dry spell was about to ensue. For how long? No one could guess.

□

Chapter - 4

For a few days, the friends and relatives kept visiting. The gravity of loss was covered in the cloak of busyness for Shantanu. After a few days, he resumed his job, but Nitin was getting engulfed in the soliloquy of his thoughts. His oasis in this desert-Sangeeta also had to return to her home. No matter how much she wanted to delay her departure, but ultimately, she had to attend the call of her duty towards her matrimonial home. Before leaving, all the while she kept on passing instructions to Nitin. In order to soothe the pain of her guilt, she kept promising Nitin that she would call him daily and he should not feel alone. As she left their house, she hugged Nitin.

There is difference between loving someone like your mother and loving thy mother. There are things one can say to his mother even when he does not intend to, but finds it difficult to say to others even when he intends to. Nitin wanted to tell her to stay, but he hesitated and held back his words. This time a tear nearly trickled from the corner of his eye and he promptly closed the door behind her.

The passing of days was getting difficult for Nitin, but the nights were even more treacherous. Sleep had completely eluded him. Often, he found his small room suffocating. His mother's memories, her thoughts and the tragic accident were all that occupied him. At nights, when breathing became difficult, he would silently get up and go out and sit on the bench of a park and keep gazing at the stars for hours. He remembered that his mother used to tell him as a child that after departing this world, the soul becomes a star. He would look at the countless stars, thinking as to which one would be his loving mother. His loss was unparallel and it was breaking him from within. His father could see that he was going downhill, but he did not know how to open the locks of his heart. It also started dawning upon Shantanu that there was only one key to it- which was now lost.

Shantanu kept making efforts to talk to Nitin, but without success. Nitin was non-responsive towards him now. Sometimes, he thought that it would be better to leave it to time, believing that time is a great healer. While at other times he thought that it might not be the best approach. He was also confused about how he should approach the situation.

One night as usual Nitin moved out of his house. A little while later, Shantanu woke up and realized that Nitin was missing. His body became tense and he panicked. Frantically, he ran towards the toilet to see whether Nitin was there. Then he quickly searched him in the other rooms. He saw that the main gate of the house was not bolted from inside. Suddenly he ran outside and started looking for Nitin. He found the watchman Ganesh, who told him that he had seen the boy sitting in the park yesterday, but today he had not gone towards that side.

Shantanu rushed towards the park and was relieved to see Nitin sitting on a bench. Shantanu ran towards Nitin and spoke in loud voice, 'Where have you been? Is this the way? What are you doing in the park at this time? Have you lost all senses?'

Nitin looked at him and then tersely looked away without responding. Shantanu was still under the grip of panic. 'What is the matter with you?' He spoke out again. 'Do you want to lose your father of heart attack now! I have been looking around for you and you are sitting alone on this bench. Have you lost your mind completely?' By this time, his voice had grown much louder and with it the simmering anger within Nitin was also growing.

Finally, Nitin's frustration reached its zenith, when Shantanu blurted out, 'Don't overreact okay... Be mature and act like grown-ups'.

Nitin responded wryly, 'How does it matter to you? Please don't act like you care for me. There was only one person in the world, who loved me, cared for me and did not judge me. She is gone and my world has gone with her'. Then he screamed, 'All her life you were killing her slowly. You are also responsible for her death. She was my mother, my friend and entire world. What was she to you? Just a person, who had to act on your commands. Move when you wanted her to, cook when you wanted to eat, cry when you were your normal self and laugh. Huh! Laugh? She never got an opportunity to smile, let alone laugh because of you. She would be much happy now that she has gone too far away from you. It's not your loss. Are you listening to me! It is mine and mine alone. I wish she had taken me along'. Then he broke into sobs.

Shantanu was shell shocked by the sudden and unexpected outburst from Nitin. Before he could come to terms with it, a barrage of verbal volleys came out from Nitin yet again. 'What did she expect from you Papa... All she wanted from you was to understand her, take care of her and take care of me. Was it too much of her to expect that you would sit with us and laugh for no reason? Why papa, why you could not make her happy? She never asked anything of you and you never understood anything about her. She has died as an unhappy person! She did not deserve this life. She was my Ma. You have always remained absorbed in your life, thinking of leading secure life, working like a machine and trying to make us machines. You would have succeeded for sure, but for her that I am still human. She and me...'. He scoffed and continued. 'All the time, I craved for love, only she was there. Every time I required guidance, only she was the one I could see. You ask me why I have come here at this time; I will tell you. I feel suffocated in that house. She may have died for you, but she is still with me. Inside that house, all the times I keep hearing her voice and her shrieks... Now will you please leave me alone!'

Shantanu was stunned to silence. He had sensed that he could not overreact. He went close to Nitin and sat near him. In the mildest possible voice, he said, 'Son, I may have proved to be a bad husband and worst father, but my intention was not bad. All I wanted was a better future for all of us. I wanted to give you a future, which I could not have. The strict discipline was only to make you a better student, believe me'.

Nitin shook his head and said, 'Ma always said that one should try to be a good person, even if he cannot be good at his work. Wouldn't that apply to studies? There is a world of difference between making rules as strict as law and developing habits to inculcate discipline. Was I ever a bad student that you had to be so tough all the times?'

Silence prevailed between them for a while. Still Shantanu could not understand that gap between them was too vast to be filled up with few soft words and he continued with his annotations. 'Look son, I can understand your agony. I too lost my parents one after the other when I was much younger than you. One has to face tremendous difficulties in life, especially when his existence itself is dependent on few morsels of bread at the pity of someone. Life teaches you how to survive in tirade of insults and abuses of your uncles and aunts who treat you like a servant only because you are dependent upon them for your daily bread. Believe me life is a great master. You will come out of this tough time, just like I did'.

The dejection in Nitin's heart was now visible on his face. He felt that for Shantanu, it was always about himself. Even in this hour, all he could only think about himself. The cocktail of anguish, abjection and anxiety was becoming too much for him. Rage took over him and he started fuming with anger. In the moment of madness, he lost complete control. 'I am sick of your silly annotations Dad! Why don't you just burn in hell...!'

Immediately after the words had escaped his mouth, Nitin realized what he had done. His entire body language changed in a moment. He could not look towards Shantanu. Even in the middle of that madness he could register the gravity of his profanity. He had abused his own father. Shantanu was totally aghast upon hearing what Nitin had just said.

Feeling ashamed by what he had done, Nitin felt like running away from the park. Suddenly he got up and left the park. Earlier he was mad at his father, but now he was also ashamed of himself. Shantanu too had never imagined that such a day would come in his life and shell-shocked by the events he remained glued to the bench.

The night sketched a portrait of a forsaken boy lost in open under the dark sky light up by thunderbolts and a miserable father who too was lost in the dark open sea.

□

Chapter - 5

The next day Nitin woke up after Shantanu had already left for his office. After having his breakfast, he was sitting idly on the sofa of the living room and he casually switched on the personal computer lying in the corner. The first pop in his mailbox was an email from Delhi College of Engineering intimating the start of first session. This mail was much anticipated moment of their lives, but now it brought a sense of relief to Nitin not because he was excited about his future, but for the reason that he wanted an escape route.

In the evening Nitin somberly informed Shantanu about the e-mail. Neither of them talked about what had happened the last night. The next evening together they went to the railway station. Nitin was taking the overnight train to Delhi. Shantanu gave last minute advices to Nitin for keeping his phone charged and to inform him promptly after reaching the campus of Delhi College of Engineering. Nitin kept nodding while the instructions were being imparted and then without saying goodbye, he took his seat in the train. He was happy to see that the shutters of the windows were already down. He let out a sigh as he settled on his seat by the window side and closed his eyes with his face looking upwards. Emotions were swelling within him, but he was unsure whether it was hatred, love or loneliness that was winning the battle within him.

Lost in his thoughts, Nitin felt the jerk of train which was starting to roll. As a reflex action his hands swiftly went across to the latch of window shutter and he pulled it up. His eyes wanted to look for someone his heart and mind did not like. In the corner stood a lonely figure of a middle-aged man who waived his hand. Finally, the goodbyes were said in signals as Nitin also waived back slightly. In the same moment Nitin looked the other way and the train crossed the platform. Strangely for himself, but Nitin felt as if he was leaving something behind.

The drama of emotions on display in the coach of train was not going unnoticed. A constant gaze was witnessing it from the moment Nitin had taken his seat. A queer looking man who had hair of a seventy-year-old, but face of a young man was quietly observing the precarious dilemma unfolding within Nitin from the upper birth seat just opposite to Nitin's seat.

After sometime when the train had picked up its express speed, the man on the upper birth came down and went towards the gate of train. Nitin too was feeling very uneasy and after a few minutes when the lights got switched off and almost all the passengers had dozed off, he too went towards the gate of his coach to catch some fresh air. The older man was smoking a cigarette. After couple of minutes, while looking outside the old man broke the silence and asked in his husky voice, 'Fresh air always helps in lighting up the spirit, isn't it?' Nitin was startled by the question, but he had not realized that the man had been observing him, so he stayed mum and just nodded. Again, silence ensued, but again after couple of minutes, the man while enjoying the last few fags of his cigarette casually remarked, 'How recent is your loss?'

Nitin felt alarmed and gave a nervous look as the old man turned around to face Nitin. Nitin sheepishly asked in return,

'Who are you and what do you know about me?'

Unfazed by the questions, the man politely said, 'It does not matter, but what really should matter to you is how you can stay happy?' Nitin gave a perplexed look. The man continued by saying, 'You must be wondering that I am a strange man, but don't worry its nothing like that. I was observing you when you came and sat in the train'.

'But how could you know so much about me just by observing, when I did not speak a word?'- retorted Nitin.

The queer looking man smiled a bit and said, 'When you will be my age, you will also be able to find out such small things, if not more'. Now his smile had turned to grin, but Nitin was not amused. 'Let me take the liberty of making one more guess, are you going to join medical college or engineering college?'

By this time, he had Nitin's full attention as his curiosity had been hyped. 'Delhi College of Engineering', said Nitin.

The man raised one of his eyebrows in arched shape and said, 'Congratulations! You must be very bright at studies'. Nitin smiled in return.

'Can I ask you one more thing, if you don't mind?' asked the man.

'Yes of course!' said Nitin spontaneously.

'Who had come to drop you at the railway station?'

'My father', Nitin said with a plain face.

'Hmm, so is the loss related to your mother or someone else very close to you?' Nitin's heart started beating faster, partly due to apprehension that he was in the presence of a person whom he did not know, but who knew a lot about him and partly because he was going through the emotional upheaval and the mention of loss of his mother was enough to trigger it. Then it struck to Nitin that this guy could be someone who is known to his father.

'Do you know my father? Are you his friend or colleague?' asked Nitin in a tense voice.

'No...No, don't get me wrong my young friend. I don't mean to startle you nor I have any intention of invading your privacy or of troubling you. It is just that I saw that you were troubled, therefore, I started chatting with you', said the old man by lifting his hands in the air, as if to suggest that he was open for the end of discussion there.

They exchanged glances and silence prevailed for few seconds. Then out of courtesy Nitin said, 'It's okay sir, it was my fault'.

'You look a lot like my son' said the man.

'Where is he?' asked Nitin.

'Far... far away, where I cannot reach even if want to'. Spoke the man in a dejected voice.

'I don't understand' said Nitin.

'He is no more in this world'. The old man had a smile on his face, but Nitin could sense the pain in his voice.

'I am very sorry' said Nitin.

'No don't be. He was a good boy. We lost him, because we or rather I could not take care of him. I could not understand his feelings, emotions and ambitions. I wish I could have that opportunity again. Every night and day I wish for it, but can't have it now. Anuj hanged himself in his bedroom'. By now, the man was again looking outside.

'I am extremely sorry sir. I think I can understand your pain. You were right. I lost my mother. She was charred to death. It was accidental fire and I tried to save her, but failed (his fists tightened and he said it with clinched teeth) and guess what? She too had a troubled life and I too wish day and night that I could get one more day to be with her, so that I could spend the entire day keeping my head in her lap'.

'First of all don't call me sir. My name is Govind. You can call me uncle Govind, if you want to'.

Nitin was so emotional by now that he could not reciprocate, but after sometime he washed his face and told his name to Govind.

Both of them did not have sleep in their eyes, so they sat on steel boxes kept near the gate. More than happiness, it is the adversity of pain and grief that pulls likes together. By this time, the commonality of their grief had woven them together in invisible thread of faith and trust.

Govind again pulled out another one from the packet of cigarettes and also offered it to Nitin who gently refused, but instead of saying sir, now he referred to him as uncle. This brought slight smile on Govind's face.

Govind: 'What hobbies do you pursue?'

Nitin: 'Earlier, I liked singing. So, one may say that it was my hobby, but now I don't like doing anything'.

Govind: 'I can understand that son. When grief overtakes us, we lose all interest, reason and sense of belongingness. But my dear, it is equally true that life does not stop. It is somewhat like a journey of train, sometimes it runs on fast mode and we take it for granted and sometimes it slows down and we grumble about it. Sometimes it halts on stations- some people get off board and some new persons come aboard. When someone pulls the chain of the running train, we start thinking that there has been a breakdown of engine and it may get stuck, but it starts its journey again.

In our lives, we have faced the last situation, but believe me the journey will start again. It is just a matter of time'.

Nitin: 'But uncle tell me what if there is actual breakdown of engine, then do we complete the journey?' He asked in a shrill sarcastic voice.

Govind smiled and said, 'Life is a journey which will only end at its destination. If the engine breaks down, then the new engine will arrive, but destination will not change due to changed circumstances'.

Nitin: 'It is easier to think about lofty principles, but it's very difficult to implement them. My mother had always guided me. Her loss can never be fulfilled. I feel doomed for all the times to come'.

Govind stood up and put his hand around Nitin's shoulders and said, 'You are right son. At the moment life would seem to come to a halt, but living life mechanically isn't anything. Life is such a big event that we cannot allow it to be wasted. We must live our lives to the best of our abilities. Sometimes it is up to us to change the settings or to press the restore button of our life'.

Nitin's eyes were glued to something on the floor of the train. Lost in his thoughts, he spoke as if he was talking to himself. 'My entire life has been constant struggle and bashing at the hands of my father. I was surviving only because of her. Now that she is gone, I don't find strength in me to move ahead in life'.

Govind: 'Loss of a dear one is incomprehensible and loss of mother is incomparable. But son, like beauty lies in the eyes of a beholder, strength and positivity also lie in the mind of beholder. We human beings have inherent tendency to live in present. We only remember the dark lessons of our past when we come across darkness again and this is how we continue to suffer the same misery again and again'.

Now for the first time Nitin nodded.

Govind continued, 'Even after having faced adversities once, we remind ourselves about them so many times that in fact we end up giving gargantuan proportions to them. Son, most of the times we fight the same battles within us over and again, in the end, these battles themselves become our biggest tormenters.

For once imagine yourself fighting with lots of people and then imagine fighting with yourself. You will find more solace in the second option. Do you know why? Because in the first situation—you don't have control over others, so the outcome of conflict is not in your control. However, in the second situation you are the tormenter as well as the victim. Both are within your control.

You have to be brave son. Don't let yourself be troubled by the same demons in your head again and again'.

Nitin looked at him reverently. 'Uncle, I wonder why my father couldn't think like you do. But, how come your son...?' Nitin could not complete the sentence.

Govind: 'Son, I have accepted it to be my destiny. In the churning of ocean, what came out first was the poison and the nectar of immortality only followed it. My son took the poison of the churning of ocean of my thoughts. Obviously, it was my failure that he had to consume it'.

Nitin realized that the pain of his son's death still troubled Govind, but he had perhaps learnt how to live with it. He tried to change the topic.

Nitin: 'Uncle what do you do for living?'

Govind smiled and said, 'Nothing'.

Nitin: 'But still you would be doing something to survive, I mean everyone has to work to earn their daily bread'.

Govind's smile became broader. 'I was in bureaucracy when my son was alive. All the time, I remained occupied with my work. The remaining time I remained consumed with the thought of maintaining my social status or for justifying the respect shown to me. Anuj's death taught me a lesson. After him, I realized that I never had the penchant for office work. My heart and soul lied in anthropology, which I had left after joining IAS. Now I am a free soul, I follow my heart and spend most of my time in tribal and backward areas of our country. As far as feeding this feeble body is concerned, the almighty who gives us the hunger pangs also makes arrangement for two morsels of roti. I have never slept hungry!'.

Nitin: 'That is amazing...'

The casual discussion that had begun with the intention to counsel the troubled young boy had turned into full discourse. Sometimes un-diverted attention has intoxicating effect on the speaker and Govind too was as drunk as a skunk by now and he started to pontificate, 'We don't realize our dreams because we lack direction, focus and belief in our dreams. Everyone around is trying to make their lives meaningful, but most people do it in bits and pieces. In a stifled manner! Some bask in the glory of the work they do, some try to feel the difference in wanderlust, some try to be poets, writers or fitness freaks and some feel the difference in performance of religious ablutions. But tell me how can the dreams, aims or ambitions turn to reality without putting our heart, mind, soul and efforts into it'.

All these words were having deep impact on Nitin. He started wondering how good it would have been, if he had opted for career in music.

In the meanwhile, outside the sun was trying to break free from the gallows of night. The light was beginning to reassert its superiority over darkness. Govind went to his seat and picked up a small bag. His destination for this journey was about to arrive. As the train screeched to halt, out of respect Nitin took the bag from the hands of Govind and accosted him to the platform. He bent to touch Govind's feet, but was stopped midway. Govind hugged him as if he was his own little boy and said, 'Son... dream, aim, love and live. Nobody can take it away from you'.

Both the gentle souls went their own way. Moving out of the railway station, Govind was basking in the deep sense of satisfaction of having done his bit to save one more Anuj. On the other hand, a new dawn was breaking in the life of Nitin.

□

Chapter - 6

The train arrived on time. Even in the wee hours, the railway station was buzzing with people. Most of the travelers had already thronged the door of the train compartment as if the wait of next few seconds was unbearable for all of them, even though they had endured the journey of almost ten hours patiently. Luckily, this was the final halt of the train. Nitin waited patiently for all the commotion to die down. A couple of coolies offered to carry his luggage, but he nodded in refusal.

Slowly, Nitin removed his luggage from the train and ambled on to the platform while thinking about the illuminating interaction of last night. The words of Govind where still ringing in his head. Lost in his thoughts he moved out of the railway station. Hordes of *autowalas* and taxi drivers were bombarding his head with offers. Nitin started feeling nauseated due to the chaos in and around him. Quickly he jumped into one auto and gave directions for going to Delhi College of Engineering.

As he escaped the frenzy of railway station, a gust of cool breeze swept through his face, but that was not good enough to ease his nerves. By this time his thoughts were dwindling between the desire of his heart and command of his mind. On one thought, he knew that if he continued on the same journey upon which he had set out, his father wouldn't let him pick up music as career. On the other hand, the thought of not going ahead was scaring him. He was sure that his true desire was to be a singer. He did not want to go ahead in joining B.Tech, but on the other hand he could imagine the angry face of his father, which was enough to send shudders down his spine. He knew that he did not have the courage to face his father without joining engineering college. However, the more he thought about pursuing a career in music, more his heart was pumping with joy. Nitin found himself to be at the crossroads of his joy and deepest fears.

Suddenly, he asked the auto driver to stop. The driver responded immediately thinking that perhaps the boy wanted to relieve himself. He was surprised when Nitin removed his luggage and paid fare to him. The auto driver tried to tell him that his destination was still far away, but with the signal of his hand Nitin stopped him in the middle of his sentence and the bemused auto driver moved on.

Nitin went to a nearby bus stop and sat on the bench under the shelter. There weren't any bystanders or waiting travelers at that hour. There were a few handfuls of vehicles on the road and couple of barking dogs nearby; but their noise was not enough to break the train of thoughts running inside Nitin's head. At last he made up his mind that he did not want to join B.Tech and had to pursue a career in music. He was done weighing the pros and cons of his career as engineer as against the career in music. He had infact made up his mind in the train last night only and now he was only convincing himself by downsizing his fears and doubts.

At his home, many a times he had seen how the singing competitions telecasted on television were tickets to instant stardom and career in music industry. The thought of winning such competition brimmed his heart with ecstasy. Still, he was aware that he had to train himself well for becoming a good singer. He took a deep breath and stopped a passing by auto rickshaw for going back to the railway station.

At that hour, the sun had almost broken out and the morning coolness of a summer day had folded into the arms of hot and sultry weather. Nitin was happy to have made a decision, but his happiness was short lived as his phone started ringing. It was a call from his father. He thought about picking it for a while, but could not muster the courage to tell his father that he was coming back without joining. The phone rang again and once again he did not take the call. He wondered why his father's decision should matter to him so much? He never cared for him and there wasn't any emotional bond left between them anyway. Nitin made a decision to free his father from this duty as well. In his mind he broke the last thread of his feelings towards his father. The unloading of the weight of broken relation relieved him. The self-given freedom liberated him from the anxiousness of stressed out ties. He switched off the mobile phone and threw it outside from the moving auto. He felt like a free bird set to explore and win the world on his own.

After few minutes once again Nitin found himself in the commotion and cacophony of the sea of crowd. Announcements were being made after every few seconds. The latest announcement was of a train to Amritsar. Nitin was lost in his thoughts. He quietly stood in the queue for purchasing ticket to his next destination about which he had no idea. All he knew was that he could not go back to his hometown, his own city or to any other city where his father had connections. He wanted to get lost forever and escape from the shackles so that his actions would not be judged or molded by his father or anyone.

It appeared as if the queue was moving by itself and the

persons at front were getting pushed ahead by themselves. Nitin was still lost in his thoughts and had almost reached the ticket counter when he felt that the lady standing in the adjoining queue was staring at him. The air escaped from his lungs as he turned to face her. The lady in blue saree had the face of his mother!

Nitin kept staring at her face with his mouth wide open. In the meanwhile, the lady in blue saree reached the ticket window and said 'Amritsar' and she turned out of the queue from the other side. Nitin was still dazed as he could not understand what had just happened and then he was pushed to the front of ticket counter where a middle-aged man with salt and pepper hair looked at Nitin. His gaze spoke of his expectation that Nitin would utter the name of city where he wanted to go. Nitin took a deep breath and said Amritsar. Thus, began his journey.

Upon leaving the ticketing counter, Nitin searched the nearby area to find that lady, but didn't see her anywhere. He kept strolling around the platform from where the train to Amritsar was scheduled to depart, but couldn't find her. At last, standing on the platform waiting for the train to arrive Nitin wondered if what he had seen was true or his mind was playing games due to lack of sleep.

After the train arrived, Nitin was fortunate to get a corner of the seat in the general compartment. It was the first time he was travelling in the unreserved general compartment of train. Very soon his focus shifted from his emotional dilemma to the awful conditions inside the train. After sitting there for five minutes, he was flabbergasted to see how people travelled in the general compartment. It appeared as if thousands of individuals had ascended into the small cabin. People were sitting on the floor. There were families who were clamoring with each other. Nitin was drenched in his own sweat. He wanted to run out to catch some fresh air, but he could not afford to leave the space occupied by him or he wouldn't get a chance to enter again. Strangely, except him no other person appeared bothered by the execrable circumstances. He breathed a sigh of relief as the train started to move. After about an hour, someone in the next cubicle started screaming and a melee ensued.

A tall, young and lean but muscular looking guy in his early twenties was slapping a thin-framed guy, who was screaming and babbling. The persons accompanying the guy who was beaten up were shouting, but strangely no one was trying to confront the aggressor. After a couple of minutes, the tall guy stopped beating as if his hand had started hurting and he quietly sat back on his seat. Then he took out the bottle of water from his bag and wiped the reddish spots on his hands. While this guy was giving unabashed beatings, Nitin had observed the reddish spot on his hand and had thought it to be bloodstain, but now it was clear that it was anything but spit of the beetle leaves, which the guy who was beaten up was chewing. A smile escaped from Nitin's lips. The commotion also settled down quickly. Nitin's feeling of malevolence turned to pity for the tall guy. The group with the thin guy also returned to their usual jabbering. Now, the entire house had returned to the normalcy of its tumultuousness.

Finally, the train reached its destination after the delay of three hours. Nitin got out of the train and scampered towards the exit gates. He was feeling sick due to the continuous heat and the stench of sweat during the entire journey. The evening had brought some relief from the soaring temperatures of the day. As he reached the main exit of the railway station, he found himself at a roundabout. Without any idea about where to go, but with resolve to move on he moved forward and saw a busy street in front with lots of hoardings of hotel and guesthouses. Towards the corner, he saw a bus with the sign of '*Shri Harimandir Sahib-Free Bus Service*'. Without opting for settling down in the comfort of air-conditioned room of a hotel, Nitin ambled towards the bus and took a seat towards the rear side of the door.

As the bus started rolling Nitin felt a rumbling sensation in his stomach. He hadn't slept for the past two nights. The uneasiness within him was rousing now. The anxiety of being a stranger in a completely new city was growing stronger. The demons of doubt and fear about the decision of starting a new life completely on his own were growing bigger in his mind with every passing minute. Then the bus stopped for a moment and Nitin saw the tall guy who was hero of the fiasco of the train getting down. In a minute's time the bus took a right turn and it halted in a busy street.

As soon as he got down, he was mesmerized by the stunning view of the Golden Temple. His giddiness made way for admiration. He was awestruck by the view of the lofty structure dipped in gold standing majestically in the night sky. Nitin lodged his luggage in the locker room and straight away headed towards the holy temple. The chanting of the holy words and the serenity of the '*Sarovar*' were accentuating his experience. After entering in the temple premises he went to the corner, closed his eyes and sat there. He could not understand the recitation of the holy verses as they were in Punjabi, but he heard the word '*Ma...*' in it and his mind drifted to the thought of his mother, whom he was missing so dearly at that time. In a few seconds the tears started rolling down his eyes and his lips were murmuring '*Ma... Ma...*'. Just then a soft hand caressed his shoulders. As he opened his eyes, he saw a lady clad in a white colored '*Salvar Kameez*' standing next to him. In a motherly tone she said, '*Putar rona kyun hain? Sab theek ho jayega! Upar wala aap hi madad karega. Rona nahi hai! Roti khayi hai tune?*'

Nitin was once again stunned. It was happening for the second time on the same day. He could not believe what his eyes were seeing. He failed to understand whether he was dreaming or was awake? The face of this lady was exactly like his mother. He kept looking at her face, while she held his arm and took him to the door of '*Langar Hall*'. She blessed him to be always happy and then moved out of his sight. Nitin wanted to follow her, but his legs froze and he could not take a step and kept standing at the same place.

After few minutes a '*Sewadar*' saw him standing near the gate and goaded him to come inside. Nitin consumed the food while his mind; heart and soul were consumed by the events, which had unfurled.

□

Chapter - 7

Nitin spent that night inside the temple. In the morning, he woke up fresh in body and mind. He wanted to share last night's incident with someone, but did not have anyone to talk to and could not take the risk of calling anyone because of the fear of getting tracked. He thought that perhaps the lack of sleep and anxiety had got the better of him yesterday, but in his heart, he felt the joy, which had deserted him for some time now. He wanted to believe, what he saw was true.

Nitin had to settle down quickly because he had only eight thousand rupees in cash, which would not have lasted too long, and he also could not take the risk of using the ATM card given by his father.

After picking his luggage, he started roaming around the temple area. As he passed near one building, he heard the sound of '*harmonium*', '*tabla*' and chorus of little children singing holy songs. He went inside and found that it was a music school. He grew apprehensive as everyone including the teacher and the disciples were Sikhs. The teacher was towards the other side of the age. He had a flowing beard which had more salt than pepper in it and all the children appeared less than ten years of age, but the sound and flow of their chorus was captivating his senses.

The class got over in few minutes and the teacher signaled Nitin to come forward. As he hesitantly approached, the teacher politely asked him in Hindi, 'How can I be of help to you?' It eased his nerves a little and then Nitin told him that he wanted to learn music, but he did not know Punjabi.

The teacher smiled gently and said, 'It does not matter, even music does not know any language as such'. Then he said, 'In music, all that matters is how pure and dedicated you are. Music does not treat anyone differently. Sa Re Ga Ma Pa are all spoken in Hindi, so you will not have any difficulty'.

Nitin felt relieved and comforted by the response. He asked, 'Guruji can you please tell me the fee that I have to pay?'

The teacher smiled again and said, 'Two hours a day. Will you be able to pay it?'

'Surely Guruji', pat came the reply.

After finding out the timings, Nitin came out of the building. Then he thought about something and hesitantly went in again and said, 'Guruji my aim is to become Indian Idol. I hope you will have no problem with it'.

The teacher started grinning. He was delighted by the innocence and respectfulness of the young boy. He was a wise man and he realized that Nitin was a good boy who had been brought up well. He took a pause and then said, 'Okay...it is good that you have told me beforehand. Now you promise me that you will not talk about this topic again until I tell you that you are ready for it'.

Nitin smiled and said, 'I promise guruji'.

Having summited his first challenge there was spring in Nitin's feet. Once again he was a carefree soul and started roaming around in the nearby '*bazaars*'. It was an old city with cramped up and busy markets. While roaming around, it struck to Nitin, that there were too many shops and stalls of eateries in the city and even more surprisingly each and every one of them were busy. Casually, he asked a shopkeeper selling women's footwear as to which one of the eateries was the best? The shopkeeper answered with vivaciousness by asking a question in return, 'what do you want to eat beta ji? We have a whole lot of delicacies in the city right from the main course to snacks, vegetarian to non-vegetarian dishes; which you will never taste anywhere else'.

Nitin was astounded by the response and he sheepishly said that he just wanted a quick bite for the breakfast. The shopkeeper then stuffed Nitin's mind with advices about what he could have, right from the '*Kulchas*' to '*Poories*' and the famous places for having them. Befuddled by the amount of information poured upon him, Nitin simply asked, 'Can you please tell which is the nearest and easiest to approach?'

The shopkeeper told him to walk straight for about a kilometer and then he will find the famous '*lassi shops*' in Hall Bazar and there were some good '*kulcha-walas*' near it.

Nitin started walking towards the desired destination and after about 20 minutes of brisk walk he reached near the two shops selling '*lassi*'. He looked around and saw the '*kulcha-walas*' in the adjoining street. Lot of people were already standing there. In a few minutes Nitin got his plate of '*kulcha*' with butter floating on top. He was extremely hungry and started gobbling the 'kulcha' even though it was way too spicy for him. A battle was raging between his hunger pangs and the feeling of abandoning it, but at last the hunger pangs were the clear winner.

After devouring his meal, Nitin took a glass of water kept in an open drum and drank it in one go. After having such a spicy breakfast, he couldn't stop himself from having sweet '*lassi*' from the famous 'lassi' shops. It was a yet another hot day and it made more sense to have a glass of cold sweet 'lassi'.

Once again Nitin had to stand in a queue and when he got his glass of the drink; it had not just cream, but a layer of butter on top of it. He was surprised to see spoon in the glass of lassi, but as soon as he took a sip, he realized the necessity of the spoon. It was actually a glass full of slightly skimmed curd with loads of sugar, cream and butter. The uneasiness of the extra spices vanished after a few sips and it tasted delicious. However, despite its taste and the euphoria attached to it, his determination started fading after drinking half a glass. He looked around and saw that two men standing next to him were gawking at him, as if they were looking down upon him for not being able to finish his glass of '*lassi*'. The thought of slipping his glass towards the used-up section disappeared from his mind. He ignored every warning his body was giving and took large sips and with every sip he took, he felt the food in his stomach coming up. With the last sip, he felt as if all the oxygen in his body had escaped. He was trying to breathe, but it appeared that the air was unable to enter in his body, as it had no space left.

With great sense of pride, he turned towards the two men who were glaring at him, only to find that they were still staring at him. At first, he thought that something must be wrong with them, but then a thought crossed his mind that maybe they were known to his father. Panic stricken, he quickly tried to move away without realizing that a cycle rickshaw was parked just behind him. As he moved, he toppled over the front wheel of the rickshaw and tumbled on to the ground only to the amusement of the bye standers and rickshaw pullers who broke into laughter. Still consumed by his panic, he did not pay much heed and briskly walked away from the spot. After about 20 meters, he turned to see if he was being followed, but saw that those men were also laughing at him. He felt deeply embarrassed for having made a fool of himself. Sheepishly, he patted his clothes and moved on.

After an hour he was still ambling in the market. As he reached near a private college his stomach started rumbling. In a matter of seconds, it became a desperate situation and he started looking for a public toilet, but to his disappointment there was none on view. He ran inside the college and frantically started searching for the loo. Few boys standing near the office guided him and he dashed towards the washrooms as fast as he possibly could. On the way, he caught a glimpse of a girl coming out of the classroom. Though Nitin was sprinting, his gaze was stuck on her face. She was trying to fix the flick of her brownish black hair. The beam of sunlight falling on her face was making her look even fairer and he felt as if her smile was brighter than the sunlight falling on her. In that moment Nitin wanted to stand there and admire her, but couldn't. After about five minutes, he came back to the same spot, but she was gone. He looked around in the whole college with the hope to catch another glimpse of her, but did not succeed.

After coming out of the college, Nitin started finding a pharmacy, generally referred to as a chemist shop in the city. He looked around in the market adjoining the college, but he could only see shoe stores or copying and printing shops. While, scolding the college authorities for not making arrangements for the urgent necessities, he found a pharmacy which was not too far away from the college. Nitin pleaded to the pharmacist to give medicine for his condition, but he refused to give the medicine without prescription. Finally, when Nitin came out dejected and had hardly walked few paces, a worker of the same pharmacy stopped him and offered to bring the medicine for extra twenty rupees. Never in his dreams had he thought that he would have to bribe someone for buying a medicine. Nitin consoled himself as extraordinary times required extra ordinary measures and readily agreed. Lo! In a few minutes he had taken the first dose of medicine procured by unfair means.

On the way back, Nitin took the route leading from the front of same college hoping to catch a glimpse of the face yet again, which was not to be. However, he saw a hand written board of a job vacancy in one of the copying and printing shops. Nitin went inside and saw a bald man with tuft of hair on all the sides of his head. He had round shaped body and he was sitting on a bench that appeared to be custom made for him. His round shaped thick moustache complimented his near perfect round structure. As Nitin introduced himself and said that he was looking for a job, the man jumped out of his bench. Nitin realized that the man was little more than five feet in height. The man also introduced himself and settled back. Although Nitin had already read outside the owner's name—Shankar Lal, but still he politely acknowledged.

Without asking anything else from Nitin, the man straight away asked, 'How much salary will you take?'

Nitin was not prepared for the question. He shrugged his shoulders and mumbled, 'five thousand'. The statement sounded more as question.

Shankar Lal leaped from his bench and blurted out, 'Do you think you are going to do the job of a professor from this shop. You kids of today think that money grows on trees and we should give away all our earnings to you'. It was apparent that Nitin's reply had appalled him. However, Shankar Lal was also in dire need of help and before Nitin could speak, he spoke again, 'I will pay you Rs.2500/- per month and a day's meal. Take it if you want or leave'.

Finally, a deal was struck at Rs.3500/- per month with the promise to increase the salary based on work performance. Shankar Lal unleashed a barrage of verbal volleys upon Nitin about the manner in which xerox copies were done.

As Nitin was walking through the streets, he thought about the days when he used to pay his monthly tuition fees of Rs.25, 000 per month and now here he was working on the annual package of about Rs.40, 000.

□

Chapter - 8

The next morning Nitin woke up to the sound of *'kirtan'*. He looked out of the window and there he was facing the majestic Golden Temple. The sun was also trying to come out of its slumber. The melodious sound of *'kirtan'* and the chirping of birds were enrapturing his senses. He stood there facing the window with his eyes closed and hands folded, till the rays of sunlight fell on his face.

He took his time to get ready for his first day at his new job and for the first music class. He took out his new check shirt and the new jeans that he had bought for attending his new college. After getting dressed properly, Nitin stood in front of mirror without any hint of emotions on his face, as if he was assuring himself that it was the beginning of the new life. The life that he always wanted!

The music class was to begin at 7'o clock, but Nitin took his seat about half an hour before the scheduled time. Slowly the students started gathering and at 7 o'clock sharp, guruji entered in the class. All the students stood up and one by one all of them took blessings from him by touching his feet. Nitin also followed suit. As he was about to touch his feet, guruji stopped him in between and gave a very pleasing smile. Nitin turned his gaze away and went back to the seat; as if he had realized that guruji had read his mind that he was touching his feet only because others were doing so.

Everybody in the class started mumbling a prayer in Punjabi. Then guruji directed all of them to recite '*Sargam*'. Nitin remained seated completely dumbfounded for the entire duration of the class. He went back very disappointed.

Nitin also reached at the shop well before the time. After about 20/30 minutes Shankar Lal came there on his old scooter and Nitin greeted him by folding his hands and politely said '*Namaste*'. Shankar Lal nodded his head in acknowledgment and went to open the locks of the shop. Having seen Nitin's clothing, he was making assessment that the boy would hardly last 2/3 days. After opening the shop, Shankar Lal asked Nitin to pull the counter on to the slab towards the outside of the shop, which he obediently did. Then he threw the broom towards Nitin. Surprisingly for him, Nitin started cleaning the floor of the shop.

Shankar Lal performed his morning prayers and then again repeated the information about the xerox machine, types of paper and small details about how to operate the machine.

There was hardly any work during the morning hours. After sitting idle for an hour Nitin realized that he had missed the breakfast. He knew that the stalls selling '*kulchas*' was just around the corner, but just then the flow of customers started coming in. Probably the 1st lecture of the day in the college had got over. Every time he thought about asking Shankar Lal's permission for having the breakfast, new customers would come in. In this hesitation, he skipped the day's first meal.

At about two in the afternoon, the flow of customers finally stemmed. Then Shankar Lal took out the lunch box and asked Nitin to join him. As he opened the box, the aroma of spices filled the air. It further accentuated Nitin's hunger pangs. He lunged on to the lunch box. After devouring 2/3 morsels of '*roti*', he realized that the dish was made of apple gourd, which he had never eaten at his home. But then he had not eaten such delicious apple gourd delicacy. Shankar Lal observed the speed with which Nitin was consuming his food and told him that four of the chapatis were for him and the remaining three were for Nitin. Even after gulping three chapatis, Nitin was still feeling hungry, but he did not have any other option except to stop.

After both of them were done with their lunch, Shankar Lal rinsed his mouth and prepared himself for siesta after giving directions to Nitin for photocopying the books. Within five minutes, Shankar Lal's snores were louder than the sound xerox machine was making. The ease with which Nitin was able to do the work was surprising for him as well. Intermittently he was looking outside towards the main gate of the college, as he was doing since morning. His eyes were trying to catch the glimpse of that unforgettable face again.

Shankar Lal was enjoying his afternoon nap and Nitin's thoughts had wondered to what his father must be doing. He was pulled out of his thoughts by the knock at the counter table of the shop. Nitin looked around and the boy who had beaten up another man in the train was standing in front of him. He gently told Nitin that he works in the neighboring shop and the owner of that shop had asked for two packets of A-4 size papers. Nitin turned around and saw that Shankar Lal was still fast asleep. The other boy understood the puzzled look on Nitin's face and said, 'Don't worry, it is a normal thing here to borrow a rim of paper from each other and you shouldn't be bothered'. He also offered to wake up Shankar Lal, but Nitin did not deem it wise to wake him up.

Nitin thought for a second and then gave two packets of papers to him. Before the other boy could leave, Nitin quickly picked up a piece of waste paper and quipped, 'Please write your name and number'.

The other boy smiled a bit, and politely said, 'Rahul and you don't need a number as you can see me going to the shop'. Nitin nodded and kept looking at Rahul who entered in the shop few meters away towards the corner of the road.

Nitin got back to his work and now he was thinking that Rahul appeared quite gentle than what he had thought of him previously. By this time Nitin was breezing through the pages of the book while doing its Xerox, when Shankar Lal woke up. He was happily surprised to see that Nitin had almost finished off the book. With a plain face Nitin handed over the rough paper to Shankar Lal and told him that he had handed over two rims of paper to their neighboring Photostat shop. Without looking into the paper Shankar Lal threw it away and murmured few rebukes for his neighbor, who was always asking for one thing or the other and would never return till he asks for it a dozen times. Nitin felt guilty, not knowing that Shankar Lal will ask for it a dozen times in the next couple of days.

After sometime the shutters of the shop came down and with it Nitin's first day at work. Shankar Lal went away on his scooter after directing Nitin to come at sharp 8:30 on the next day. As Nitin passed the neighboring shop, he saw Rahul locking the shutter of his shop and momentarily thought about stopping there, but he hesitated and moved on. There was spring in his steps and a relaxed smile on the face. His day had gone well and he was feeling happy about it. Walking through the streets amidst clangor of the sounds of variety of vehicles, he felt that he belonged to this place.

□

Chapter - 9

The next few days breezed past quickly. Nitin had got settled into the routine of attending the morning music classes, skipping his breakfast, having three chapatis with Shankar Lal, doing xerox copies and eating '*langar*' at night. In a matter of few weeks Shankar Lal had developed faith in Nitin and every now and then he used to leave the shop to Nitin for hours. Nitin had understood the simple nuances of the business and customers were also happy to deal with him. Many a times even in the presence of Shankar Lal the customers called out Nitin to explain the portions they wanted to get photocopied. Shankar Lal wondered that perhaps youngsters wanted to interact with people of their age, however, he failed to recognize the true reason; he always had a plain face while interacting with customers and Nitin used to greet everyone with a smile.

One afternoon, Nitin finally got some free time and Shankar Lal was enjoying his mid-day siesta. Feeling bored he picked up question papers of physics that he had xeroxed about an hour ago. The first question paper that he picked up fascinated him. The unusual questions of the paper aroused his love for physics and he picked up the waste paper sheets and started solving them one after the other. The more questions he solved, the more intrigued he felt to solve the next one. Lost in solving the questions, he did not realize that he had breezed past almost all the numericals in under an hour. As he was about to solve the last question suddenly Shankar Lal's snores stopped and while rubbing his eyes he got up from the bench. On seeing Shankar Lal getting up, Nitin hastily kept the rough paper sheets of solutions in the same set of question papers.

As soon as Shankar Lal got up he gave some money and keys of his scooter to Nitin and sent him to the market for buying rims of papers. Nitin had no option but to obey him. On the way to market and back his mind was absorbed by the thought that if Shankar Lal discovers those sheets, he will obviously realize that he was very well educated. There was a serious threat of his discovery, which could jeopardize everything for him. In his zest to return quickly, Nitin was accelerating the scooter to its limits. Drowned in his contemplation, he failed to register the presence of traffic police officer. In a flash, the police officer signaled him to pull over to the side. Nitin pleaded with him to let him go, but his requests failed to make any impact and Nitin had to endure the delay of 15/20 minutes.

After coming back Nitin tried to locate the question papers and the rough answer sheets, but they were gone. He remained tense through out the day expecting Shankar Lal to pop out a question to him about the answer sheets, but when the day passed without any such event, he thanked his stars for the lucky escape.

In the evening after closing the shop as Nitin passing by, he saw that the shop where Rahul worked was already closed. He moved on in to the myriad of streets. By now, he had discovered the shorter paths.

Feeling lost about the day's development, Nitin was going through one such dark street. As he took a turn, he saw a pack of street dogs standing right in the middle of the deserted street. He looked at the dogs and shuddered a bit. In order to avoid the pack he turned around and started pacing quickly. As he took the turn backwards, the dogs started barking loudly. Even though Nitin had his back towards them and could not see what was happening behind him, but instinctively he knew that he was being chased by the pack of street dogs. In no time, he was sprinting in the small streets, which were almost deserted. As the pack reached his heels, Nitin jumped on to a high slab at the entrance of a house. In the moment of despair and being scared to death the sympathetic nervous system of his body had got activated and his body was in flight or fight mode. Nitin's eyes quickly scanned the area around for picking up any object, but when he couldn't find anything to lay his hands upon, he raised his empty fist in the air as if he carried something in it and then flung it towards the dogs in such a manner as if he was throwing something at them. It worked for a moment as the pack retreated slightly, but the dogs did not move far away for Nitin to escape and now the dogs knew that he had nothing in his hands.

In desperation, Nitin started shouting loudly and frantically at the dogs to keep them at bay. Upon hearing the outcries, the lights of few of the houses got switched on. Nitin was oblivious to it; in those few seconds no help came forth. When it seemed to him that the attack on him was inevitable and his shouts were only making the dogs more aggressive, his hopes started evaporating and he was getting mentally prepared for being bitten and attacked. Then from the corner of his eye, he saw a boy coming out of the dark with a stick like object. The boy swung the object i.e. a cricket bat close to the dogs, but it missed them. He also let out a loud shout. After being attacked, the pack of dogs ran away as quickly as they had come.

Nitin was drenched in sweat and he was trembling. He

was so shaken up that for few seconds he did not realize that the boy who had saved him and was asking him to step down was 'Rahul' only. Rahul got Nitin to sit on the slab and signaled to other people who had come out on the street to go back, as everything was fine.

Nitin had become so numb that though he could hear the voices around, but his mind was not able to process any of it. The next second he saw a boy of his age rushing towards him with a glass of water in one hand and a string of prayer beads in the other. After sipping some water, Nitin felt relieved. Rahul had put a hand on his shoulder and was trying to pacify him. Finally, Nitin responded that he was fine and had not been bitten by the dogs.

Rahul asked Nitin to come inside his house for a while. Though Nitin hesitated, but Rahul insisted that he should rest for a few minutes and then he will walk him through to his destination.

As Nitin followed both the brothers to their house, he saw that Rahul's brother was sporting a long tuft of hair at the back (a *Shikha*) and had smeared '*tilak*'(clay marking) on his forehead. Both the brothers resembled each other a lot, but the younger one was three/four inches shorter in height from Rahul and had a petite body as compared to the muscular structure of his elder brother. However, his complexion was fairer than that of Rahul.

Few feet inside the house a small staircase led to the first floor. The house had a small courtyard of about 10 square feet with one room towards the right side and a kitchen and one toilet. Towards the corner of the house, there was another small enclosure, which could hardly be described as a room.

Rahul and his brother led Nitin to the main room, which had bluish colored walls. It was crammed up with things all around. A small girl of about 12 or 13 years was sitting at corner of the double bed near a closed window which probably opened towards the outside of the house. There was a chair and a stool in the room. Nitin took the chair, Rahul sat next to him on the stool and Rahul's brother sat on the bed. The interiors of the room were simple, neat and clean. A television set was lying on a table in the corner of the room opposite to the bed. The pictures of gods and goddesses were also kept on a small shelf in the middle of the room. One photograph of a man with a plastic garland in front of it was hanging on the other side of the room.

Before anyone could break silence, Rahul's mother came from the kitchen. Nitin stood up from the chair and folded his hands in 'Namaste' to greet her. She too responded with a smile and a nod. Rahul introduced Nitin to his mother and told that he works near his place. She stood there briefly and told Nitin not to worry and again went inside the kitchen. Then Rahul's brother introduced himself as 'Arjun' and he folded his hands and greeted him by saying, '*Radhe-Radhe*'. The little girl sitting in the corner also shyly nodded her head in greetings.

After the introduction got over, Rahul asked Nitin how he had got there in first place? In response Nitin said that he was trying a shorter path for going back to the '*Sarai*'. Arjun intervened and said that it almost cost him very dearly and then all of them broke into a gentle laughter.

Rahul's mother called out to his sister, 'Sonia'. In a minute, Sonia was back in the room with two plates containing '*roti*' and '*dal*'. She placed one plate in front of Rahul and the other before Nitin. Nitin hesitated and said that he will have it in the '*Sarai*', but Rahul insisted and he could not refuse it. After a long time, he was eating a home cooked dinner. After going through his meals, Nitin picked up his used plate, but Arjun took it from his hands and with a smile on his face said that he was their guest. Nitin said goodbye to everyone in Rahul's family and on his way back, he was joined by Rahul.

On the way back, Nitin thanked Rahul profusely for coming to his timely aid and for the sweet gesture of his family. Rahul told him not to think much of it. He then pointed out that taking shortcuts at odd hours is never a good idea. Rahul casually told Nitin that earlier he had seen him in the train and in the bus from railway station to the Golden Temple. Nitin smiled and reiterated the episode of train and what he had initially thought of Rahul. Then both of them had a hearty laugh about it.

While enjoying each other's company they reached the front gate of the Golden Temple. Though Nitin did not have to go to the '*langar hall*' today, but he did not feel like missing his evening visit to the temple. He offered Rahul to join him, but Rahul rebuffed it bluntly. Nitin had started feeling that a bond of friendship was developing between them, but Rahul's unexpected response took him slightly aback. Rahul sensed Nitin's uneasiness and said, 'It was a personal choice he had made some time ago and he does not visit any temple or religious place'.

Before leaving, Rahul asked Nitin if he will be able to go back from there by himself or should he wait? Nitin felt slightly chagrined at this offer as it implied that he could be afraid of street dogs, but his irritation soon vanished when he thought of the affection and concern which caused Rahul to make such an offer. He smiled and said, 'Can I call you bhaiya?' Now it was Rahul's turn to be taken aback and hesitatingly he said, 'Why not brother?' Nitin hugged him and said, 'See you at work tomorrow bhaiya'.

As both of them were about to turn around, Rahul spoke

again, 'You said that you are staying in a '*Sarai*'?'

Nitin responded by saying, 'Yes'.

'If you don't mind, since when are you staying there?' asked Rahul.

'Ever since the day you saw me on the bus' said Nitin and then he smiled.

'Then I am sure that you won't be able to stay there for long' said Rahul.

The 'Sewadar' of the 'Sarai' had already asked Nitin, on couple of occasions as to when he was to shift. He thought a bit and said, 'Of course not too long'.

Rahul promptly responded, 'I had thought so too... I was wondering, if you want a place to stay? We have one vacant room at the first floor'.

Nitin was bowled over by the offer and he almost felt embarrassed by the magnanimity of the offer. Though he had thought that may be Rahul could suggest some good place for him, but it did not occur to him that he would invite him to stay at his own home. He stuttered and said, 'No...no... please you have already done enough for me. I can't be a burden to you or your family'.

Rahul threw his hand around Nitin's shoulder and said, 'It will be no charity brother. Our tenant, who was occupying the room on the first floor, had vacated it about a month ago and you can pay the rent. He used to pay Rs.1300/- per month to our mother. You can pay the same'.

Now Nitin felt at ease, but before he could say anything, Rahul spoke again, 'You can think over it and tell me later. There is no need to rush about it and we don't have any person already lined up for renting it out.'

Nitin nodded and said thanks to Rahul again. Both of them smiled at ach other and went their own ways.

On his way back, Rahul was recapitulating the entire chain of events and it took him no time to assess that Nitin was a nice boy from a well of family. The sequence of events had already made it clear to him that Nitin had probably run off from his house. A nice, well-dressed and well-behaved boy travelling in unreserved compartment and then working for a paltry salary at the photocopying shop meant nothing else. He had felt warmth for Nitin. He felt as if Nitin had probably made a soft corner for himself in his heart much earlier and today's incident had only provided a spark for him to make that offer.

On the other hand, while taking a round of the sacred '*sarovar*', Nitin's mind was also engulfed in the thoughts as to how their destinies had worked to make them meet each other time and again. How he had met Rahul in the train, then in the bus and later at work place. How today's incident had brought him to Rahul's doorsteps and that too when he came out completely unscathed! Till this day, he was all-alone and a stranger in a new city, but now he had the opportunity to stay around Rahul and his family at their home.

Walking around the temple, he had reached near the '*langar hall*', where he had seen his motherly figure telling him that all will be well. In his heart he was convinced that his mother was still watching over him. She had not abandoned him! With a smiling face and teary eyes, he knelt towards the sanctum sanctorum of the temple and folded his hands in deep gratitude to god or to his mother, he did not know!

□

Chapter - 10

The next morning, Nitin packed up his clothes and bid goodbye to all the '*Sewadars*' of the '*Sarai*' and took his entire luggage to his music class. The class had already begun. The smile on Nitin's face was brighter than usual. Guruji understood that he was going to someplace new for which he was very happy. It felt as if the sweet bird had found a nest. However, as usual guruji did not start conversation about it with Nitin. He was not the kind of person who would begin a conversation with anyone about his or her personal issues unless he was spoken to. He gave a smile back to Nitin and signaled him to sit and then looked at the clock. It was the first day when Nitin had gotten late for the music class and he had completely understandable reason for it. Nitin quickly took a seat in the class and started singing along with others.

After the class got over Nitin went to guruji for customary taking of his blessings and told guruji that he was shifting to a new place. Guruji smiled and said, he hoped that he would not be late anymore again.

Nitin instantaneously responded with utmost reverence by folding his hands, 'No...No... guruji not again'. And both of them smiled.

Nitin took a cycle rickshaw and within ten minutes he was at the door of Rahul's house. After few knocks at the door, Arjun opened it and he was surprised to see Nitin with luggage in his hands. Awkwardly Nitin told him that Rahul had asked him to take a room on rent. Arjun brought him in and as they entered the courtyard, Nitin was greeted by the surprised faces of Rahul's mother i.e. Poonam Aunty and Sonia. Nitin got embarrassed as it became apparent that Rahul had not informed his family members about their discussion of last night. Sonia went inside and woke up Rahul, who came out still rubbing his eyes and then took the luggage from Nitin. As they moved towards the staircase, Rahul told Nitin that he should have informed him so that he could have got the room cleaned at least.

Going upstairs Nitin could hear Arjun telling his mother the reason why he was there with his luggage. Nitin realized that he had acted hastily, but now he had no other choice. It was a small room of 8 x 12 feet. A wooden folding bed was kept in the corner. There was a small gallery towards the side of the room, which opened to the side of courtyard of the house. The walls of the room were painted with light yellow color. Nitin told Rahul that he will take care of cleanliness and he shouldn't worry. As Rahul went downstairs, Nitin picked up a small broom kept outside the room and cleared the cobwebs in an otherwise clean room.

After about half an hour, Rahul called Nitin for having breakfast, but Nitin politely refused by telling a lie that he had already had his breakfast. He did not want to look shamefaced again. After few minutes both Rahul and Nitin went to work together. The cost of that lie was that Nitin had to skip his breakfast, as he could not have stopped for eating '*kulchas*' from a stall with Rahul by his side.

The day went by and in the evening, Nitin asked Shankar Lal for permission to leave a little early. Upon coming to know that he had shifted to Rahul's place, Shankar Lal flung out his usual rebukes for his neighboring competitor. Then he said to Nitin that instead of falling in trap of those scoundrels, he should have told him, if he wanted a place for rented accommodation. Nitin knew that there was no point in explaining anything to him, so he kept quiet. Shankar Lal ended his monologue by saying that now he should stay there for a month or so and in the meanwhile he will find some better place and at a cheaper price for him. Nitin understood Shankar Lal's misplaced insecurities, but he was in a hurry and without getting into argument with him, he quickly left the shop. While leaving he stopped by Rahul's shop and told him that he will be coming back separately. Rahul too gave final pieces of advice regarding the places from where he could buy his stuff.

Nitin reached home late at night. He had bought couple of white bed-sheets, a glass jug, steel glasses and toiletries etc. Rahul helped him in transporting those things to his room. The day's work and evening shopping had left Nitin exhausted. In the busyness of his shopping spree he had forgotten to eat something along. Now he was too tired to go out for having food. He thought of taking some rest and as soon as he fell on the bed, exhaustion took over and he fell asleep. However, hunger didn't let him sleep for long and he woke up in the middle of the night. There was no possibility of any '*dhaba*' or eatery to be open at that time. He went back to the bed hoping to fall asleep, but kept tossing and turning. The howling of dogs only made it worse for him to sleep. He came out to the terrace for catching some fresh air. It was the first night when he had to go hungry.

Arjun too had woken up and was taking bath before sitting for his daily meditation. As he came out of the bath, he saw Nitin leaning on the wall of the terrace and out of curiosity he went upstairs. Nitin was looking at the stars and he did not realize that Arjun was standing behind him. Arjun softly called his name from behind. The moment he said 'Nitin', Nitin instinctively jumped ahead and screamed. Arjun also got unsettled and looked around to see if they had woken up others or not? Lying on the ground Nitin saw Arjun and felt like shouting at him, but he controlled his anger.

Nitin took Arjun's hand and got up. Arjun apologized for startling him and asked what he was Nitin doing at that time?

Nitin chuckled softly and said, 'Brother you could have found some other way of asking this question as well...You almost gave me a heart attack'.

Arjun too smiled and then said, 'I again feel sorry brother...I saw you leaning over the wall and came up to ask if everything was fine'.

Nitin answered while leaning on the wall again, 'Yeah... got up some time back and wasn't able to sleep again. So thought of coming out'.

Arjun said, 'Change of place...hmm?'

Nitin answered, 'Don't know may be...or may be because I had skipped the dinner'.

They looked at each other and smiled. Arjun patted Nitin on his back and took him to the kitchen. They found four bread slices, but nothing else. Arjun said in irritated tone, 'Rahul Bhaiya doesn't leave anything'. Nitin signaled that even this would do. They toasted the bread and put some ghee and salt on it. Nitin checked the time and it was not even four.

Both of them went upstairs where Nitin devoured the slices of bread and asked Arjun, why he was up so early? Arjun told him that it was his routine of getting up early for meditation and chanting.

It surprised Nitin a little, but now the smearing of '*tilak*' and keeping of *'shikha'* made sense to him. He thanked Arjun, who took his leave and entered the small room in the courtyard and Nitin went back to his room to have sound sleep.

The next morning, Nitin woke up to the sounds of *'Tulsi Aarti'* and *'Tulsi Pranam Mantra'*. He saw that Arjun was offering prayers to a flowerpot of *'Tulsi'*. He saw his wristwatch and it was about 5:45 am. He silently thanked Arjun for waking him up, otherwise he would have missed the music class again as he had forgotten not to set his alarm.

Now slowly everything was falling in place for Nitin. He was attending music classes, had a job and also a place to stay. Nitin wanted to put his best step forward and devote maximum time to music classes. One day after the music class he asked guruji if he could attend evening classes as well. His entreaty was politely turned down. Guruji rather told him to rehearse his lessons properly at home, but on seeing the dejection on his face also added that he was always welcome to come to the academy for practice in the evenings as well. Nitin nodded in agreement. In any case, he had to come to the Golden Temple for daily darshan and for having *'langar'*, which had become his daily routine.

The week passed by in a jiffy. The morning and evening walks from home to work and back with Rahul were becoming more and more enterprising. He was learning a lot about the city and of course about Rahul as well.

On one of the usual days while Nitin was busy in doing Xerox copies two college students came to the shop and asked Shankar Lal about the solved paper which they had found in their Xerox copies. Hearing this, bells started ringing in Nitin's ears and he saw his worst fears coming to reality again. Finding no way out, Nitin dug his head in the Xerox machine and kept copying the papers blindly. The sheets coming out of the machine were overlapped copies, but Nitin did not have any clue about it.

The boys were trying to show the answers written on the waste paper sheets to Shankar Lal, but he kept avoiding it. Instead he kept reiterating that they must have got it mixed up somewhere else, as there was no one in his shop who could solve it and there was also no chance of mixing up of papers because no other person had come to ask for it. Then Shankar Lal turned around and asked Nitin if anyone had come to ask for any such sheets? Nitin's heart was pounding and without turning around he answered, 'No'. Shankar Lal laughed and asked those boys to keep the material, if they liked it. Both the boys looked towards Nitin, who had not turned around since they came. They picked the notes and left.

After the boys had left, it took Nitin more than ten minutes to calm himself down. He was expecting Shankar Lal to ask more questions about it. His last few minutes had gone into making all sort of possible explanations for what had happened. However, he thanked his good fortune again that Shankar Lal did not raise the issue. He was convinced that Shankar Lal did not doubt that it could be him.

By that time Nitin had done lots of photocopies where the subject to be copied was either missing or was crisscrossed. Realizing that he was doing the work blindly, he quietly began the work again without Shankar Lal getting to know about it.

Nitin tried to conceal his distress throughout the day and felt that he had succeeded in hoodwinking Shankar Lal. On the way back, he was quieter than usual. Reluctantly Rahul asked him, 'Is everything fine with you?'

Nitin replied, 'It isn't anything. May be some bug is troubling me since morning.'

Rahul shot back- 'Oh... I thought maybe you were agonized

by today's incident of students proclaiming that you were a genius'.

Nitin was stunned and he almost turned pale. While looking away Rahul continued in his normal casual tone and said, 'I think you are getting these bugs from the food which you eat outside.". He turned towards Nitin and said, 'I think it will be better if you start having meals at home, just like the earlier tenant used to. This way you will be able to stay healthy and my mother is a very good cook. She can turn inedible vegetables like bitter gourd into delicacies'. Then he continued to sing praises of his mother's culinary skills as if nothing had happened. He added, 'But you will have to pay more'.

Nitin was so thunderstruck that he could not say anything except for smiling and nodding. He was trying to stay calm from outside, but inside him a storm of mixed thoughts was raging furiously. He was completely bewildered, whether Rahul believed story of students or not? In this hour of dilemma Nitin chose to stay mum about it and more than the choice it was actually due to lack of his discernment about what was happening. Then just like that Rahul changed the topic of chat to another mundane incident of the day.

That evening Nitin did not go for the evening practice class or to the Golden Temple. He slouched in his bed thinking about what had happened, till Arjun knocked his door and asked him to join for dinner. The moment of utter chaos had also brought another change in his daily life. Now he was having a simple dinner with family again.

On the other side of the town, at the terrace of his house, Shankar Lal was just tossing and turning in his bed. Sleep was eluding him today. His wife Rajni was observing him since he had come back from the shop. She went closer to Shankar Lal and asked, 'What is the matter? You don't seem too well. Is everything all right? Should I bring something for you?'

Shankar Lal turned towards her and affectionately looked at her round face with black brown eyes and sharp nose. Oil was dripping from her black hair on to her forehead, which made her skin shine in dim light of night. Then he let out a sigh! 'No. I am just fine. I don't need anything'.

'Then what is the matter? Something is troubling you that I can see'. said Rajini politely.

'I told you there is a new boy in the shop, who I had employed'. Before Shankar Lal could complete his sentence, Rajni interjected. 'Has he stolen something or is he taking drugs?' There was panic in her voice.

'No... no... its nothing like that Rajni. Atleast hear me before jumping to conclusions'. Shankar Lal said to her in irritated tone. 'He is too good a boy for such things'.

'Then what is it?' Asked Rajni.

'There was always something about the boy, which was slightly strange'. He paused and looked at Rajni who was now listening intently to him. 'From the looks he appears to be belonging to a well-to-do family. The clothes that he wears, his watch and his overall mannerism are not of any usual boy who works at a photocopy shop. I have always wondered that there is something missing about him. Perhaps he is hiding something'.

'They may have fallen to bad times, just like so many families do'. Responded Rajni. 'Have you not talked to him about it?' She added.

'No, I have actually never got a chance to talk to him about something like this. I have talked to him about you and also about our children many a times. He always listens, but he has never ever said anything about his own family. Normally a person who has recently fallen on tough times will take the first opportunity to talk about it, because his pain and anguish overpowers his thoughts most of the times. Something like this happens only when a person wants to hide something'. Said Shankar Lal in a strained voice.

Rajini put her hand on Shankar Lal's shoulder and said in a doting tone. 'Shankar there are people who do not like to share their feelings or conditions with anyone. You do not over think about the situation'.

'You are not getting it!' countered Shankar Lal. 'Today two boys came up and said that someone from our shop had solved the test series of D.C.Verma. You know that being long in this business, I certainly know that those are not easy tests. His tests actually make the students cringe'.

'Do you think that this boy Nitin solved it?' Asked Rajni quizzically.

'No, I don't think so. I know that he did it! He started behaving strangely the moment I asked him about it. He continued to make copies cryptically for long time. He thought I did not notice it, but I could clearly see from the corner of my eye what he was doing'. His voice was becoming denser with every word he spoke.

Rajni almost gasped upon hearing that her husband had let the boy make wrong copies for so long, but then her expressions changed and a smile escaped from her lips.

She knew her husband well enough to know that he had developed affections for this boy or he had clothed himself with the caring mantle for this boy. She kept quiet and Shankar Lal continued.

'He thinks that I don't have a hunch that he has fled from his house. He feels as if his mask of lies is intact. Little does he know that truth cannot remain hidden behind the facade of lies for long'.

'So what have you thought? Will you talk to him?' Asked Rajni.

Shankar Lal sighed again. 'I really don't know. I am certain that if I talk to him, he will run away from here as well. On the other hand, he is too good a boy to be wasting his life like this. Sometimes, I wonder how his parents had instilled such goodness in him and how could a boy like him leave them at all or maybe he has done something sinistrous that he had to go into hiding'.

Rajni realized that her husband was in dilemma whether to talk to Nitin or not. Being an outsider in the situation, it was easy for her to grasp that Shankar Lal was in no position to help Nitin the way he wanted to. She squeezed her husband's shoulders a little more and said, 'Relax dear... from whatever you have told me, I don't think he would have done something bad and if he had done something like that, then so be it. See a lie which does not hurt anyone, is not a lie after all'. She caressed his forehead and smilingly said, 'You don't trouble yourself... you give him some time. Maybe he will tell you his story by himself or at least by that time you will be able to convince him about his own good'.

Then very slowly she said something, which completely eased up Shankar Lal. She said, 'Correcting someone is the most devilish task. Right now, if you tell him what he needs to do, then he will not take it and you cannot tell him what he wants to hear, because it may not be good for him. So now your job is to wait for the right moment and then you can talk to him about his own good so that he can see for himself, what he actually needs to do. Then it will be up to him to make the decision. These are the kinds of decisions that determine one's destiny!'

Shankar Lal took her hand away from his forehead and

gently wrapped it in both his hands and said, 'Yes, you are right my dear. Maybe it's better, if I stay quiet for now and continue to help him in the small ways I can'.

The growing darkness of the night was able to settle the dust of the daylight. At one side, Nitin had fallen asleep wondering, what tomorrow had in store for him. On the other side, Rahul also had gone into slumber without troubling the chords of his heart and mind. Shankar Lal too fell asleep in the lap of night, which was swaddling him like a mother now and his wife was watching him sleep in peace.

□

Chapter - 11

The days passed by as usual. Every morning Nitin would be at the shop before Shankar Lal. Now he had resigned to the niggling desire of catching the glimpse of that face again.

A week after the incident, while walking back to their house, Rahul laughed and made a jovial remark that the word of Nitin being physics genius has spread and very soon there will be locks on every other copying shop. Nitin smirked that it was all the imagination of his mind. But, he very well knew that there was considerable increase in the flow of work since the last few days.

The next day at noon, while Nitin was taking a tea break he saw 'that girl' coming out of the gate of college. She was wearing a '*Salwar Kameez Suit*'. Her hands were constantly fixing the 'dupatta' on her shoulders. Nitin's gaze was totally fixed on her. When she reached very close to the shop, he realized that she was coming straight towards him. Upon climbing stairs of the shop, she moved towards Shankar Lal and handed over the sheets of papers to him, who further handed it over Nitin. Nitin was completely dazed. He had never experienced butterflies in his stomach and pounding of heart at the same time before. In a mechanical manner, he got up and got the copies done and handed them straight to her. His eyes were glued on her, but once again she completely ignored him, gave money to Shankar Lal and went back towards the gate of the college. Then she sat on a scooty, which another girl was holding for her and left. Shankar Lal patted on Nitin's shoulder and pointed towards a cup of tea lying in front of him.

In the afternoon before starting his lunch Nitin sprinted towards Rahul's shop and then ran besides the counter straight towards him. His happiness was uncontrollable. Rahul looked at him, smiled and said '*What?*' Nitin grinned and rolled one of his eyebrows upwards and also moved his neck along with it. He caught hold of Rahul shoulders with both his hands and said, '*Bhaiya ji! Ho Gaya, it's done!*'

Rahul too grinned and said, 'What happened- *kya Ho Gaya*?' Nitin gesticulated in a dancing motion and said, 'She came to the shop today'.

Rahul nodded and said, 'Ok... we will talk about it later or your employer will come after you'.

Nitin ran back. No doubt Rahul was right, Shankar Lal enquired from him about the reason why he had gone to Rahul's shop. He scolded Nitin slightly to show his displeasure, but it did not affect Nitin. He was on cloud nine.

Going back home, Nitin was animated in describing the day's incident. Rahul finally had to say, 'Mr Romeo it's ok..., she visited the shop just for her work'.

Nitin - 'Bhaiya you don't know. It's been so... long since I was waiting to see her'.

Rahul- 'Fine... now don't start again. I have already heard that silly incident enough times'.

At home, after having dinner, Nitin did not feel like going back to his room and he was still afraid of going out alone because of street dogs. He saw that Rahul was glued to the television set, so he looked towards Arjun and asked him, if he wanted to go for out for a stroll. Arjun picked up his bean bag and motioned his hand towards Nitin signalling him to move.

It was pleasant outside. A strong breeze was blowing, which was a relief from the summer heat. A few minutes passed in silence. Then realizing that he will have to start the conversation, finally Nitin asked, 'What is there in the bag that you are holding?'

Arjun explained, 'I am a follower of Krishna consciousness and there is a string of prayer beads in it'.

Nitin apologized to him, 'I am sorry for having disturbed you in your prayers'. Nitin had seen that Arjun's hand was moving inside the sack.

Arjun's shoulders drooped slightly and very humbly he said, 'Not at all dear. The recitation of god's name continues for us throughout the day. Even at work, I keep doing it along with other daily chores. Don't worry I wouldn't have joined you, if I wanted to meditate only'. The answer relaxed Nitin.

'Every morning I see you rushing before Rahul bhaiya goes for work. It reminds me of the days when we used to go to school…always rushing'. Arjun said with a smile.

Nitin guffawed and said, 'Yes, I do go to a school, but it is a music school and I go to learn singing. In fact it's my passion'. He looked at the stars in the sky and said, 'In fact, it is my dream to become Indian Idol someday'.

Arjun responded, 'Oh sure! God willing you will achieve your dream one day. You know music is very dear to god. Sri Chaitanya Mahaprabhu attained divinity by expressing his love for god through music only. Srila Prabhupada has also shown the same path. I too go to 'Kirtans', but unfortunately do not know how to play any instrument nor I am good at singing, so I just join the choir. God knows may be one day you will teach me how to sing well'. Then he burst into laughter.

Nitin went on to ask, 'How you manage to keep the bean bag with you throughout the day and how are you so dedicated towards Krishna consciousness at such tender age?'

Arjun smiled and said, 'There is no age for loving Krishna the ultimate God, my friend. It is just how and when he touches you. If you go to Krishna temples in Vrindavan, you will find that children of tender ages have become devotees. It is your karmas of past and present life, which decide your path in the present life'.

Nitin was impressed by the maturity and poise of Arjun and he also felt embarrassed for asking a silly question. He tried to cover up and said, 'I meant to ask, at what age you came in contact with this mission?'

Arjun answered, 'It's been more than two years now. I had got admission in the college, which is right in front of your shop. On the day, when I went for taking admission, book distribution was going on outside the college. I took one book and after that I started going to '*kirtans*' regularly'. Then with all the calmness in the world, he said, 'It has been my savior'.

Nitin guessed that Arjun was saying it metaphorically for spiritual gains, but before he could think any further, Arjun said, 'After the passing of our Dad, all we could see was darkness around us. It has showed me the light at the end of the tunnel. It not only gave me the hope and strength in that moment, but also showed me the real path for eluding the darkness forever'.

'Is the daily practice not quite tough?' asked Nitin while curling his eyebrows in arched shape.

Arjun smiled again, 'Nothing is tough, if it becomes the purpose of your life. It becomes a joyful journey. The love of God takes the raft of your life through the rough waters like you are sailing smoothly on a boat. You tell me, do you find taking your music classes or doing rehearsals tough at times?'

Nitin replied. 'No, but I don't know about others who have

to listen to my rehearsals'.

Both of them chuckled. Then with serenity in his voice, Arjun said, 'I am sure you would be a terrific singer, but there is a good saying in our mission, we do 'kirtan' for ourselves and not for other people. Since, we sing the praise of God for our love for him, it does not matter to us as to what others think of it. Believe me, even if others do not enjoy our singing, they cannot miss out our love for singing the grace of almighty and it certainly connects'.

Nitin was being floored by Arjun's eloquence. He was wondering, how mature Arjun was for his age and then Arjun said, 'I think you should also join us for 'kirtan' on some days. I am sure everyone will love to hear you'.

Nitin nodded and said, 'Certainly. I will go with you, but you have to promise that you will not insist upon me to sing there'.

Both grinned again for umpteenth time that evening. Then Arjun said, 'I think we should be heading back or else mother will send Rahul bhaiya to save both of us fearing another attack of street dogs'.

As they reached home, while going upstairs Nitin saw that Arjun went inside the small room towards the corner of the courtyard and realized it was the den of meditation for Arjun.

That night Nitin went to sleep not thinking about the 'revenant extraordinaire' which was the highlight of the day, but about the evening well spent with a new friend. He was beginning to doubt himself, wondering how differently Arjun had acted in almost similar situation that he too was in. At last, he slept with the realization that everybody is different in his or her own way.

□

Chapter - 12

The following day while coming back from work, Rahul sensed that Nitin was quieter than usual and he was not discussing anything about his previous days incident. He asked, '*Did you see her today?*'

Nitin shook his head in denial.

Rahul smiled and sarcastically said, 'So, now you have had the realization that your crush is over?'

Nitin too smiled and said, 'No...no... it is not'.

Rahul again jovially asked, 'Don't tell me that you are getting serious about her. Tell me smart boy are you thinking of eloping with her'and he bursted into laughter.

Nitin scoffed and said, 'Would you stop making fun of me now. On the one hand, I have not seen her today and on top of that, you are making fun of me?'

Finding Nitin slightly relaxed, Rahul finally said, 'Did Arjun say anything to you last night?'

Nitin was surprised and said, 'No...No, nothing special. We just discussed about his interest in God and stuff like that'.

Now, it was Rahul's turn to scoff. He sneered and then paused for a moment and said, 'Listen to me buddy and don't take him seriously. He can be a little weird at times'.

Nitin gave animated response and said, 'No, it was nothing like that. Actually, I found him to be a very nice and kindhearted person and very mature too'.

'Mature, my foot!' exclaimed Rahul and then continued. 'I know he is nice and kind, but not mature. Denying the realities and remaining in fool's paradise is not maturity. It is escapism! When the moment to act strongly came, he succumbed and went into his own reclusive world. Life does not pass just on beliefs. He became one of those fellows who close their eyes like pigeons in front of cat and then believe that cat will also not see them'.

Nitin fell silent. For the first time he was sensing that there were deep rooted differences between the brothers. Rahul had still not ended and he continued. 'Had it not been for our mother, he would have gone to the hermitage long time ago and leaving all of us in lurch'. He sighed and spoke again. 'May be there is some part of you which I wanted to see in him, but couldn't. Tell me, how can someone think of leaving their family members when they need him the most?'

Rahul had grown so comfortable with Nitin that he did not feel the necessity of hiding his feelings before him. Nitin too felt the pain in Rahul's voice. In order to soothe Rahul, he said, 'It's ok bhaiya. Everybody is not the same'.

'There can be no justification for it brother'. Rahul said in a hardened tone and determined voice. 'When our father passed away, the entire family was in turmoil and he decided to leave everything for becoming a full time devotee. Mother was already finding it difficult to cope up with loss of one family member and lo, he disclosed his decision to her and that too privately. She almost went into shock. Had it not been for Sonia, God knows what would have happened to her. He did not even think of our little sister. She is too young to have suffered the loss of father at such tender age and he wanted to give another shock. To be honest, I think she is braver and stronger than Arjun. At the age of eleven, she took care of mother when I was away at work. Had she not acted responsibly after the death of our father, mother would have drained herself in flood of tears'.

Rahul had become very tense. Nitin tried to pacify him. 'All is well that ends well. He is finally settled and back at home'.

'Finally! Mother had a brain fade when he told her that he was going for good. She had to be hospitalized. The doctors told him to pacify her and that is when he promised to her that he will not go till things get settled'. Rahul curled his lips and continued, 'He was such a good boy, an obedient son, a loving brother and a very good student. Then one day somehow he came in touch with these missionaries and his entire mind got washed'.

Nitin said, 'Don't you ever talk to him about it?'

'Yes, of course I did! Not once but many times. Now I have come to realize that you cannot convince someone who does not want to listen. Though he had stopped that day, but he will go, of that I am certain. No one knows his definition of settlement of things, not even he himself'.

The pain troubling Rahul was clearly visible on his face. He was feeling frustrated about having lost his brother already. Rahul was truly the elder of the family now. He wanted to protect everyone, but was feeling helpless.

At that moment, Nitin decided to end the discussion as it was only tormenting Rahul. He requested Rahul to forget it and said, 'Leave it Bhaiya...Now only good things will happen as the worst is over'. Rahul was not the kind of person to stretch the discussion, which was too personal for him.

They had reached 'hall bazar'. Nitin changed the topic and pointed towards the 'lassi shops' and narrated the old incident of the time when he had landed in the job with Shankar Lal. Nitin was trying to laugh, but Rahul wasn't amused. Still Nitin continued in vain to cheer up his friend.

During the night walk with Arjun, Nitin asked him, 'Why did you decide to become a fulltime devotee? '

Arjun paused and then looked straight into Nitin's eyes and said, 'So bhaiya has told you about it?'

It occurred to Nitin that Arjun might be feeling offended by his question and said, 'I am sorry, I didn't mean to intrude in your personal life, but I have come to respect you I and I couldn't understand why you didn't talk to Rahul bhaiya about your decision and its reasons more clearly'.

Arjun rejected his apprehension and said, 'No brother, you are also like a family member, so please don't apologize. Regarding your question, I think there is no point in explaining things to a person who is not ready for it. Rahul bhaiya has no love for God at the moment. How can you explain the matters of heart to a person who uses his mind to understand it? I love and respect my elder brother a lot. He is a very good man, but I also know that he is not prepared to understand my thinking and point of view'.

Nitin felt a duty towards Rahul to convince Arjun about his point of view and said, 'See my dear friend, we all understand that there is a time for everything. Probably the timing of your decision was more disconcerting to him'.

Arjun again smiled and said, 'You have understood his version of things about mother's breakdown etc. It is not the complete truth. I admit it was my mistake as our mother was not prepared for it, but my love for Krishna Consciousness was known to everyone and even to our beloved father. He was still undergoing treatment, when I had brought books from the book distribution. I used to read 'Bhagavad Gita' to him also. He never disapproved of my love for Krishna rather he too developed the love for Krishna in his last days.

It was not immediately after father's death that I decided

to become a full time devotee. It was almost six months after that. Having seen the end of father, my heart was beating for love of Krishna. I had become certain that this circle of pain and pleasure will only end at the feet of Supreme deity and for that I had to follow the path. I had to do, what I had to!'

Nitin still tried to persist in his endeavor of trying to remove the differences between both the brothers. 'May be bhaiya thinks that the missionaries had swayed you'.

'Rahul bhaiya is a very kind hearted soul, but he also acts impulsively. It is nothing but the product of his imagination. You know when I saw mother in that condition, I felt concerned, but I did not feel the pain for I knew that man proposes but God only disposes, so whatever was happening was due to the will of the Supreme authority. However, it was my 'Swamiji', whom he calls a missionary, who told me that now was not the time. He also told me that my time will come, but only when I have discharged my duties. Now what would you say?' answered Arjun with poise.

Nitin had no answer to it. He had always curbed his instinct of asking about their father's death. Asking such questions meant exposing himself to similar questions from them, for which he himself was not prepared. In those moments the friend's pain was overpowering his instincts of preserving his secrets. On most occasions a person's mind loses its battle with heart, not just in times of personal grief, but also when he is touched by other's pain. In that instant he felt a strong bond with Arjun.

'How did uncle pass away?' Nitin finally gave in.

For the first time he saw sadness in Arjun's eyes. 'Dad fought a battle with cancer and he lost it. He had cancer in his food pipe. It was detected when he couldn't swallow food anymore'.

Nitin asked in somber voice, 'But then, it could have been detected on time. Weren't the doctors able to detect it?'

'Our father was a teacher in a private school. Being a man of limited resources and unlimited responsibilities, he avoided going to see the doctor till it was very late. Bhaiya was studying in B.Com 2nd year'. He added with smile, 'and I was in Xth standard. The draining of resources would have played on our father's mind. Even after confirmation of malignancy, he did not go for treatment to Delhi or Mumbai, because he had to take tuitions. Going to these places meant that he couldn't take tuitions and he wasn't certain if school authorities would give him sick leave for the period of treatment. He did not last all his chemotherapies'.

Arjun stopped and sat on the footpath. Nitin was slightly startled, but he did not have any other option, so he also sat along with him. Now both of them were sitting on the footpath of main road of Gandhi Gate. Arjun's voice was growing dense as he continued to speak, but his eyes weren't moist anymore. He spoke again, 'You know, sometimes I feel that more than the disease it was his worry which took him away. He was always concerned about our future after he is gone. How will we study or even survive? The day it was confirmed that he had cancer, he went to bhaiya's room, sat next to him and almost cried. He said to bhaiya, you don't worry; I will make some arrangements for you guys. Getting costly treatment and paying our tuition fees was an extremely daunting task. He tried to save every penny he could. He used to commute to hospital in a pooled auto rickshaw, whereas, he was required to take much more precautions.

I accompanied him to the hospital on some occasions and he would always ask the doctor, how much time he had in this world? The doctor never responded. On the day, when he got the last chemotherapy, the same doctor told him 'Sharma ji...you have just one more session of chemotherapy and then I guarantee you ten years'. He was so happy at dinner. He told us not to worry and everything will be sorted out. He was supposed to take proper rest, but he continued going to school and from there he picked the viral flu, which turned into Asthma. Then he couldn't recover. He passed away on the day of his scheduled appointment for last chemotherapy'.

He paused for few seconds. Now, Arjun did not feel any desire to hide his old grief from a newfound friend. 'After father's death, we did not have any source of income as all of us were into studies at that time and mother had never stepped out of the house. She had always been a house maker. Then we learnt that father had taken debt for his treatment from local moneylender.

One day, the owner of 'Sai Photostat Shop' came for bereavement and out of regard for our father, he offered a job to Rahul bhaiya a job and he dropped from college and took up that job. Later on, the school authorities also offered a job of peon. Mother also joined the job, but her health deteriorated and she could not pursue it. Bhaiya insisted that I should continue with my studies, but I knew there wasn't any money to support my studies even if my fee was waived. Against his wishes, I too dropped out from the college. Our father's friend Ramesh uncle talked to someone and got me this job'.

'Do you intend to resume your studies through correspondence or something now?' asked Nitin.

'It is not possible either for me or for bhaiya to do it. The debt is too heavy and we are hardly able to pay the interest even though bhaiya does other jobs as well, of which even I don't know'.

Nitin was also surprised, 'Other work? I didn't know, if he

was doing any other work?'

'He goes out of the city for 2/ 3 days every month for his other work. Anyhow, that is the long and short of our story my dear brother. Now you tell me, how do I convince bhaiya of my actions? My actions are for myself only and I suppose my responsibility is to see through our family through these rough waters'.

Both of them remained silent for the remaining part of their track back home. Upon entering the house, Arjun again went back to his small room and Nitin to his own.

Nitin's head was spinning due to the long discussion he had with Arjun. He couldn't help but think about both the brothers who were born and brought up in the same circumstances, but yet were poles apart personalities. Thinking about them, Nitin felt that everyone has his own way of thinking. Perhaps there is no such thing as absolute right/wrong or absolute good/ bad and maybe they are only the manifestations of our own believes.

The loss of a family member had torn him inside out, but these guys were holding on to each other in much difficult circumstances. It made him feel that amidst all the tension with the outside world and within them, both the brothers had something which he did not have i.e. the bond of love of family members. The beautiful desire to protect each other, to care for one another and to pull themselves out of the mess together.

For the first time he started doubting his own decision of leaving the house. He began to see that may be there was some connection between their lives and his own. Thinking about lives of his two good friends made him think about his own life too.

□

Chapter - 13

Nitin's life was following a template now. Waking up on hearing the sound of '*tulsi aarti*' and in case he still faked sleeping, Arjun's knock on the window used to put him out of bed. Poonam Aunty would always impress upon Nitin to have his '*parantha's*' before leaving for music class. After sometime, she had started insisting that no one should leave the house without having breakfast. It meant additional work for her so early in the morning, but in any case, she had to cook food for Sonia who also left for school at the same time.

Attending classes, remaining busy at work, catching glimpses of her- whose name was still unknown to him, evening chats with Rahul on the way back, usual laughter and banter at dinner and then finally singing session on the terrace before his sole audience i.e his friend Arjun. The last ritual of the day was often the most amusing of all for him.

Nitin would sing various songs while Arjun would tap his hands on the old wooden bench which was also the seat of their jamming sessions. Upon completion of each song, Arjun used to give his comments. After his mother there was no one in Nitin's life who could come up and tell him, where he was right or wrong without being judgmental about him. In absence of such a person in life, it was so easy for him to get swayed without knowledge of his imperfections. The role of such a person is extremely vital for progressing as he/she keeps one grounded. Arjun was filling the boots of becoming that person for Nitin, whose presence was so important for him for leading a balanced life.

Nitin knew that with Arjun his actions would not be judged. This knowledge not only made him stronger, but also made their bond even stronger. Nitin was able to accept his advice easily because he was aware that it wasn't being given due to any feeling of superiority, but only because of sheer desire of his welfare.

Nitin often laughed to Arjun that they were forging a bond of '*Krishna*' and '*Sudama*' and both of them were incomplete without the other. On one such occasion, Arjun reminded Nitin that there is always a '*Sudama*' in everyone's life with whom that person shares the pure bond of love. Nitin considered himself lucky to have two such persons in his life Arjun and Rahul.

Slowly Nitin became a regular at '*kirtans*' with Arjun. With time he was promoted as a lead singer and that too without Arjun's intervention. Everyone in the group had developed fondness for him and Nitin also liked them.

At other fronts, Rahul had made Nitin buy a smartphone. While buying the SIM card, Rahul had given his own personal details. He knew that Nitin did not have any identity proof of Amritsar and he did not want to embarrass him by asking about other identity proofs.

At work Shankar Lal was itching to increase Nitin's salary, which was a rare incident in the entire duration of his working experience. No doubt the work had increased many folds, but he was insecure that Nitin may want to leave although Nitin had not said anything of the sort to him.

One day Shankar Lal pointed towards the old and unused desktop lying in the corner and said, 'I think we should make use of the computer too. The name of the shop also needs justification'.

Nitin went out and saw that the board of the shop read, 'Computer Printing and Photostat Shop'.

Shankar Lal remarked, 'I think we need to find a new boy for computer work. Then he looked from the side of his eyes and asked, 'I suppose you wouldn't be much computer friendly?'

By now young boys and girls of the college had openly started asking Nitin if he was the same guy who had solved D.C.Verma sir's test paper series perfectly. So, Nitin also had an idea that Shankar Lal knew well that he was well qualified and therefore he was asking him indirectly. Sometimes it is difficult to accept a simple development or a new thought upfront, but then even the most arduous situations become more palatable if they are laid to rest for a while. With time Nitin too had grown comfortable with thought that it was fine even if Shankar Lal or others knew that he had solved the paper. The passage of time had given strength to his thought that nothing will happen even if they knew.

Very comfortably Nitin said, 'No, I can work on it, but I don't think this computer set will work. It is very old and its hardware and software won't work. We will have to buy a new one'.

The idea of making investment for buying a new PC was dissuading for Shankar Lal. However, after a day's rumination he decided that pros of buying a new computer were more than the cons for not buying it. At last, he along with Nitin went to the market and instead of purchasing a PC they ended up buying a new laptop. Nitin had told him that this way he will be able to work from home as well, if required.

Slowly the days started getting busier and free time was

hard to come by for Nitin. Shankar Lal too had started working equally hard for photocopying as Nitin was mostly occupied with computer printing work. Shankar Lal had increased his salary to Rs.4500/- p.m. now.

The visits of 'the girl' had become more frequent. One day Nitin learnt her name, when one of her friends had called her out loudly- 'Mehak'.

Coming back from work, his discussions with Rahul revolved around Mehak. Rahul was finding Nitin's behaviour bemusing. He kept pestering Nitin to atleast talk to her, but Nitin always shrugged away by saying, 'Why does he want to shatter his notions?' and then he would break into laughter. Rahul often repeated that at least it would save him from the drudgery of listening to his one-sided love story.

They had kept note of the time when Mehak used to leave from college and Nitin would discreetly look at her. He could not muster courage to look her in the eye. One day Nitin was occupied with work and Rahul came near his shop and called him out loudly. Nitin leaned over from the counter. In order to signal him to look towards gate of the college, Rahul swayed his neck towards the gate of college, but Nitin failed to understand what he was trying to tell. Rahul repeated it twice, but finding that Nitin was not getting it, he raised his hand and pointed towards Mehak, who was riding the scooty straight towards their side. As Nitin turned his neck, a smile escaped from Mehak's lips. In the comedy of errors, Nitin jerked backwards to avoid being seen and fell back from the counter. After she had passed, he got up and frowned at Rahul who was laughing hysterically. Nitin would have almost yelled at him, but could not do so due to presence of Shankar Lal.

The evenings passed juggling between practise sessions

with Arjun and going for walks with him. After that Nitin would often sleep working on his laptop. In addition, looking at Mehak's profile on Facebook and Instagram was one of his favourite time-pass activities.

Rahul kept pestering Nitin to at least send a friend request to her on Facebook. Nitin himself had not put his picture on his own Facebook profile. One night, Nitin thought to himself that what difference will it make if he sends a friend request to her, as she would not know who he was? Half asleep he pressed the send button. For next few days, he kept watching if the friend request had been accepted or not. After 4/5 days, he felt demoralized and became sad. Rahul tried to cheer him up by saying that there can be several reasons other than her lack of interest for him. Maybe she isn't too active on Facebook and in any case he had done the dumbest thing by not putting his photo on the profile picture. Gradually, Nitin stopped discussing Mehak in their evening chats.

One afternoon, Shankar Lal had gone to market and Nitin was doing his copying work. A middle-aged man in his early fifties, who was wearing a normal pant shirt came to the shop. He had long curly hair which had not been cut for last few months. He was wearing rectangular spectacles, had a moustache and probably had not shaved for 3-4 days too.

He called Nitin and gave him few papers and asked if he could copy them on priority. Nitin nodded and courteously took papers from him, as he did with all the customers. In a span of five minutes, Nitin handed over the xerox copies to him. While he was returning the change, the man asked him, 'Are you the boy who solved my test series?'

Nitin could not understand the import of question and said, 'Uncle, what did you say?'

The man replied, 'I am D.C.Verma, the professor of physics.

I had heard from my students that you had solved the question paper of my test series. Is it true? Was that you?'

Nitin politely said, 'Sorry sir, I did not know that you were D.C.Verma sir. I have heard a lot about you from many students'.

The professor asked again, 'Son, you have not answered my question?'

Since, Shankar Lal was not around and Nitin had practically accepted that everyone knew that it was him who had solved the paper, he did not find any necessity in hiding it. Moreover, he also wanted to know, what was so special in that test series that it had become such an issue. He politely but firmly said, 'Yes sir!'

The man remarked, 'Well... I saw your answers and they were mostly correct. At first, I was not ready to accept that a boy working on photostat shop could do it. The last time any student solved it like you did, he was amongst the top rankers of IIT'.

Now Nitin had the answer to the query in his mind and he blushed at the compliment. D.C.Verma continued speaking, 'Whatever be your story, I am not interested in knowing it. I have come here because the guy of such competency should not be wasting his time at photo copying papers'.

Nitin felt thrilled at such compliments coming from a person who was considered to be the best teacher of physics in the city and whose students regularly got selected in IIT's.

Physics was always his favourite subject and it was because of his score in Maths and Chemistry that he could not crack the IIT.

D.C. Verma again spoke, 'Look, I think you should come and join my coaching institute. You will earn much better than here and most of all you will not be wasting your talent'.

Nitin came out of the shop and quickly asked, 'But sir,

what will I do in the coaching centre, I mean you are already there to teach?'

D.C. Verma answered sternly, 'Of course, I am there, but there are many other things to do in a coaching centre. You can upgrade the course material, provide assistance to our online candidates and in case, if I find you good enough, then you can take the clarificatory classes as well'.

Nitin fell silent. It was the offer he had never anticipated. It did look extremely lucrative to him, but the suddenness of the offer had baffled him. D.C. Verma understood his predicament and said, 'Don't worry. You may take your time and respond later. Here, take my visiting card. You can call me or come to the coaching centre, if you wish too'.

Nitin folded his hands in respectful manner and took his blessings. After about an hour, Shankar Lal came back, but Nitin did not tell him anything. He was aware of Shankar Lal's insecurities towards him and did not want to trouble him until he had made a decision.

On the way back, Nitin shared the day's development with Rahul. Rahul did not look surprised. He thought about it and after a considerable pause said, 'What was the exact offer that he made to you?'

Nitin responded, 'Exactly, as I told you'.

'Then you should ask him all the details like salary etc. But more than that are you comfortable about it?'

Nitin said, 'I don't know. Leaving Shankar Lal uncle in lurch does not feel right'.

Rahul tried to impress upon Nitin. 'It's important for you to think wisely. You have to work at either of the places. You may ask for little time to join the coaching centre. The salary there in any case would be much better than what you get here and to be honest the work of coaching centre will also be better than here. Anyways you are not going to do photostat work for your entire life and there is no question of leaving anybody in lurch. It is plain and simple understanding; you don't have to be too emotional about it. Rather I am very happy that you have got this offer'.

Nitin exhaled and remained silent.

At night, Nitin did not go for the walk. He sat with Arjun on the terrace, but today he wasn't rehearsing either. He shared his dilemma with Arjun.

Arjun asked, 'Do you feel that you will let Shankar Lal down by joining the coaching centre?'

Nitin looked at him and then turned his face to the other side. He knew that somehow Arjun always found a way to read his mind.

'Have you told your uncle about the offer?' Continued Arjun.

'No'. Pat came the reply.

Arjun said, 'If you ask me, I will say that it is a very difficult choice. On the one hand you have a person with whom you share a bond of trust and friendship, so much so, that mere thought of leaving him is draining you. On the other hand, you know that you can't be with him forever. Actually, why don't you tell him about the offer and then see his response. Maybe it will be of help?'

'How can I do it?' said Nitin. 'Right from the beginning he has always been very protective and caring for me. Recently he has started a new venture by relying upon me. You should have seen him counting the money while purchasing the laptop. The poor guy must have parted with most of his savings'. Nitin paused for a second as he felt a lump developing in his throat. 'He increased my salary on his own. It has never happened with him before. Tell me, why would he do it? Obviously, he cares for me a lot. I can see it on his face. You know, I have a feeling that he has started the new work just for me! Brother, he treats me like a son and how can I leave a father like...'. Nitin could not complete his sentence for more than one reason. 'If I tell him about today's incident, he will think as if I am wanting to leave him. I can't do that to him'.

Arjun looked at Nitin and smiled. 'My dear friend, I think you don't know, but you have already made the decision. In the battle between your head and heart, your heart will never lose. You are blessed my dear brother'. He placed the palm of his hand on Nitin's head. Then he said, 'Come on don't worry! As you said the other day, there is always a time for everything'. He reminded Nitin of his own advice given to him a few days ago. Then enthusiastically Arjun said, 'We will not go to sleep without a song and in any case you are going to be a famous singer, so you will have the chance to make up for the lost money'.

Nitin shook his head in nay.

'Ok', said Arjun. 'Then, I will have to do the honours and he sang the 'bhajan' of 'Krishna' and 'Yashoda maa'.

The next morning, Nitin did not tell Shankar Lal about the visit of D.C.Verma. Rahul kept coming to their shop to meet Nitin. Everytime he quietly asked Nitin if he had told Shankar Lal about it or not? Nitin kept procrastinating.

The next few days on their walk back to house, Rahul kept trying to convince Nitin to accept the offer. One evening Rahul was very irritated. He had told Nitin several times that he was making a mistake. Such a good offer had come to his door steps and he shouldn't let it go begging'. He even tried emotional blackmailing by saying that, 'You say that I am your bhaiya, but you don't treat me that way! You are no different than Arjun. All of you make such foolish decisions and you will remember my counsel once you find yourself in tough situations. You guys live in a dreamland. Money is the most vital aspect of life'.

For a moment, Nitin saw a glimpse of his father in Rahul, but he knew that Rahul loved him and he was disturbed only for his betterment. He also knew that Rahul was not going to give up, so he kept saying that he hasn't decided and will very soon do.

As they had reached near the street leading to their house, two persons riding on a motorcycle came from behind and stopped just in front of them. The one riding the bike was a huge guy, having thick moustaches and was wearing a stud in his ear. The other person sitting on the pillion rider's seat looked like a bodybuilder. The guy riding the bike opened a packet of chewing tobacco and while putting it in his mouth said, 'What Rahul, you are not returning the loan and you have also stopped visiting the office?'

Nitin got very scared, but Rahul maintained his composure. With a straight back and slightly dense tone he retorted, 'I am paying the instalments that we had agreed'.

The man smiled and turned his face and looked at Rahul. By placing his elbow on the handle of the bike, he said in a threatening tone, 'We had agreed on other things also. Why aren't you coming to the office? You know it better son. Come to the office tomorrow'.

The threatening tone added fuel to fire. Anger raged within Rahul and he retorted angrily, 'I am making the payments. Don't try to threaten me and I will come to the office when I want to'.

The man on the rear seat got down and tried to catch hold of Rahul from the collar of his shirt, but before he could pull Rahul down, Rahul swung and caught hold of him from his neck. Nitin was so terrified that he almost froze. He would not have been able to run even if he was attacked. However, the big guy at the front seat of the bike yelled at them and hurled abuses. He got off and with a jerk he untangled his associate. He signalled his associate to go back towards the bike. Then he came up close to Rahul. He was six inches taller than Rahul and he looked into Rahul's eyes and murmured, 'You know what you have to do now!' and they left.

Nitin and Rahul stood there watching the bike as it rode past the street. Nitin was in complete shock, but Rahul was still panting with anger.

After they left, Nitin wiped the sweat of his forehead and asked Rahul, 'What was it? What did just happen?'

Rahul responded, 'Nothing. They are the goons of the money lending company to whom we owe debt. They were bugging me with phone calls for last two days and now they have sent these boors. Anyhow, I know how to deal with them. You don't tell anyone at home or they will get stressed about it'.

After a pause, Nitin said, 'I have saved some money, you take it if you want'.

Rahul said in exasperation, 'No matter how much we repay, the loan will always be there'. Then he looked at Nitin and while patting his back said, 'Don't worry little brother, I will manage it'.

Walking towards their home, Nitin was in awe of Rahul. The man had not flinched for a moment when Nitin couldn't move. He asked, 'Bhaiya, were you really not afraid at that time?'

Rahul grimaced and said, 'There are times in life when you can't afford the luxury of being afraid. These people are blood hounds, if they smell fear, they will pounce upon you'.

Nitin asked again, 'Have you always been like this? It requires lot of courage to stand up against such people the way you did today. I could hardly move'.

'Adversities make you the man you are. When you don't have any other option, then you become what you are required to be. Had Dad been alive, I would have also reacted just like you'.

They had reached the entrance of their house. Rahul signalled Nitin to keep quiet and they went inside.

That evening Nitin learnt another lesson in the chapter of life which was new to him. He understood another meaning of family's love. The strong unspoken bond due to which a person like Rahul was facing so many things all alone for the sake of his family without letting them know about it. His respect had increased manifold for a boy who had turned into a hardened man in the face of adversity.

□

Chapter - 14

Arjun was slowly losing his appetite for some time and he was also losing weight gradually. His mother was getting concerned, but Arjun would casually avoid discussing it by brushing aside her concerns on lame pretexts. He was eating lesser and lesser with each passing day. Rahul had also scolded him once or twice about it, but when Arjun did not pay any heed to his advice, he stopped interfering. Nitin too tried to persuade him to eat more, but Arjun always responded that he didn't feel like eating more.

After about two weeks, Nitin got up in haste and realized that he had overslept for more than one hour. As he went downstairs, he saw that Rahul too was awake, which was unusual. He came to know that Arjun was having high fever since last night. Early in the morning when his mother had gone to his room, he was drenched in his sweat and was shaking. Since morning they were treating him with ice packs.

Nitin quickly went outside and brought an auto rickshaw. With the help of Rahul, he took Arjun to the dispensary. The doctor gave medicines and prescribed number of tests. They spent the entire afternoon in getting the tests and X-rays conducted. He had skipped his music class and work for the first time.

They continued the treatment for two days, but it did not bring any relief. After two days Rahul and his mother again took Arjun to see the doctor. After examining all the reports, doctor told them that Arjun was having Tuberculosis and lymph nodes had developed in his body. He required aggressive treatment for almost a year along with complete bed rest for few months.

In the evening, when Nitin returned home, the mood at home was sombre. Arjun had developed high evening fever by that time and was lying unconscious. Poonam Aunty was sitting in the corner. She was sobbing and cursing her fate. Rahul too looked crest fallen and was lying on the bed. Their little sister Sonia was changing the ice sponges from Arjun's forehead. Nitin went close to Arjun and checked his fever by placing his hand on his forehead, which was literally burning.

Sonia was the first to break the silence. 'The fever is very high, but with iced water sponges, it will come down very soon'.

Nitin nodded to her. Then he came to know about Arjun's diagnosis from Rahul. It came as a jolt even to Nitin and he did not know what to say.

Finding everyone's spirits deflated, Sonia was determined not to appear worried in front of her dispirited family. She spoke with aplomb. 'We all should know that it is a completely treatable disease. All he needs to do is to take his medicines regularly without fail. There is nothing to be so worried. He will be fine'.

Nitin was gobsmacked by the positivity shown by the little girl. He supported her, 'You are absolutely correct Sonia, the fever will go away in a day or two and then in a month or two he will be completely fine'.

In the evening no one could eat their meal. Nitin and Rahul were sitting on the terrace. Rahul was very disturbed. 'Don't worry bhaiya everything will be fine', said Nitin. He felt that the news that his brother was inflicted with a deadly disease was very painful for Rahul.

'I just pray that he gets well. Then he may do whatever he wants to do with his life'. Rahul eyes became moist as he uttered these words.

Nitin had seen Rahul so emotional for the first time. A complete atheist was talking of praying for his little brother. He discerned that in the event of life and death situation, all the differences that Rahul had spoken about so aggressively had vanished in thin air. At this stage, his love for his brother was paramount and all he wanted now was his good health and long life. It was as if love for his brother was making way from the hardened heart of Rahul like a small sapling does through the crevices of a rock, but on the second thought, he found that he was again wrong. There was never any love lost between them! In this moment, the pretence of false egos had fallen and their decisive misunderstandings had turned out to be trivialities. Like in so many families around, their strong faith in their respective opinions was turning out to be a masquerade which did not last long in the moment of truth.

Arjun's fever went away in two days. Nitin started spending his evenings by Arjun's bedside. It came as a relief for Arjun's mother and his little sister. Nitin used to tell him the stories of his days' work or read holy books to him or they just watched television. In a week's time Arjun's fever had gone, but his frail body was extremely weak. He could hardly walk down to toilet without someone's help. The doctor had advised him to take high protein diet which included eating animal protein. Arjun could never accept animal food and he did not even eat eggs. It flabbergasted Rahul and mostly he stopped short of yelling. Often, he said, 'Bhai... there must be some animal protein in your medicines as well'. However, Arjun always maintained silence and did not respond. Ultimately all of them had to be contented with him eating lentils and drinking cow's milk.

Arjun's recovery was slow and in three weeks' time Nitin started taking him upstairs for offering the morning prayers to '*tulsi*'. Arjun had been removed from the job and this had added additional burden on their otherwise tottering financial condition. The next month Arjun's salary did not come and they found it difficult to pay their normal bills and Sonia's school fee could not be paid as well.

Rahul took up additional work of computer printing from his employer. He used to borrow Nitin's laptop and would type the documents till late night. Nitin's typing speed was better than Rahul's, therefore most of the times Nitin took Rahul's typing work as well by telling lies that he required the laptop urgently and thereafter he used to complete the work for both of them.

Nitin was there with all of them for some part of the day and their condition was not hidden from him anymore. His heart ached to see them in such a condition. He was aware that Rahul would never accept any kind of financial help from him. Nitin used to bring groceries and quietly hand them over to Rahul's mother without Rahul knowing about it. Still he knew that he could do a lot more, but was unable to. The feeling of helplessness was making him despondent.

In order to lighten his burden of helping them financially, Nitin thought of increasing the rent of his room. He knew too well that if he tried to increase it straight away, then they would never accept it, but will rather feel offended. The next Sunday, Rahul had gone to the office of money lending company for settling the account and Nitin and Sonia were present in the room with Arjun. While chit chatting, Nitin intentionally tried to bring the discussion to the point where he could offer to increase the rent. He looked at Arjun and said, 'A boy in the market was saying yesterday that rates of rents have gone sky high. That boy had recently shifted to a one room set for the rent of Rs. 3000/- per month'.

Arjun was listening to him inattentively. Nitin continued, 'I think you could have got a better rent from your earlier tenant as well'.

Arjun gave him a perplexed look and said, 'Earlier tenant? Which earlier tenant are you talking about buddy? You are the first tenant in this house'.

Nitin was gobsmacked upon hearing this and both the brother and sister looked at his agape condition and then they looked at each other. It was obvious that Nitin was utterly surprised.

'Is everything alright?' asked Arjun.

'Yes, no... I mean, wasn't there a tenant in the room which I am occupying right now?' asked Nitin hesitantly.

'No, it used to be bhaiya's room. But why do you ask?' said Arjun.

Nitin tried to control himself. This new discovery had left him so astounded that he forgot the purpose for which he had started the conversation. It also occurred to him that despite innumerable chit chats with Arjun, the mention of earlier tenant had never cropped up.

'I must have misunderstood it' said Nitin and went out of the room.

The next morning, while coming back both Nitin and Rahul were silent. After reaching half the distance, Nitin asked in acerbic tone. 'Why did you lie about the earlier tenant story bhaiya?'

Rahul smiled slightly and said, 'What should I say? You were new to the city and was staying in a '*Sarai*' for so many days. You needed help and I kind of liked you'.

'Who told you that I was a stranger in the city?' asked Nitin by slightly raising his voice.

'What do you think? You are behaving as if I am a fool. You were there in the train from Delhi. The next day you land up in a job of photostat and then you are going to the Sarai! What other sense does it make except for the fact that you had run away from your house'. As the last words escaped from his mouth, he turned towards Nitin who was completely shocked.

'Did you know all along that I had fled from home?' asked Nitin slowly.

Rahul realized that in his frustration he had made a mistake. He had let out a secret which he had harboured for months. He held on to Nitin and said, 'Look Nitin, I am sorry! You are as dear to me as Arjun and I will not let any harm come to you. I have never asked you nor will I ask you about the reasons for anything related to it. It is your space and I completely respect that. As far as your question goes, it was pretty obvious my little brother'.

Rahul held Nitin's face with both his hands and lovingly said, 'You have such a pure heart. Standing outside the Golden Temple, I made a decision to help you and when you said can I call you bhaiya? I knew I could always trust you as a brother'.

Sometimes the show of acrimony is also a way of displaying hurt and Nitin was trying to do that only, but could not continue with the role play for long and he hugged Rahul. 'I don't know how to thank you bhaiya! You have always been there for me since I have come to the city and you sacrificed your room for me... a complete stranger'. Nitin was speechless for sometime. Emotions were swelling up within him, but he managed to pacify himself and spoke again, 'Come what may, you will always find me next to you! Still I have one grievance against you'

Rahul gave him a bemused look. Nitin uttered again, 'You say that I am your little brother, but you don't let me make any contribution. Am I not a part of your family!'

The expressions on Rahul's face hardened and he looked away and then said, 'It's not that Nitin. I know you love me and you feel that you are part of family, but it just doesn't seem right. You are already paying rent and more'.

Nitin turned towards Rahul and by looking him in the eye, he said, 'Didn't Arjun contribute his salary? So, tell me... don't you treat me like Arjun?'

For the first time Rahul did not have any answer. He sighed and said, 'Ok. You too contribute. From now on I will not stop you'. His answer brought a boisterous smile to Nitin's face.

Rahul pushed Nitin and urged him to move on. 'Now move, don't you want to go home today. Your friend Arjun would be waiting for you and for your Gita reading session'.

They smiled and moved on. After walking for few paces, Rahul asked Nitin, 'Tell me how is your singing and practice going on?'

'Wonderful'. Pat came the reply.

'Great, I saw the advertisement of start of new season of reality singing shows on TV. Are you ready for it?' asked Rahul.

'I too saw the advertisements and I asked guruji if I was ready?' Said Nitin.

'What did he say?' asked Rahul.

'I was pestering him with this query again and again after the classes and one day he said to me, look son I think you have progressed well, but I don't think you are ready for it yet'. Answered Nitin with dejection in his voice.

Rahul suddenly remarked in protest. 'You should have asked him the reason. You have been practicing so well for the last many months and you sing well. In fact,much better than most of the guys, who appear on those TV shows. Does your guruji even watch such TV shows?'

'I don't know'. Responded Nitin.

'Then what is the harm in atleast trying. There are no fixed chances for participating in such shows or is it so? We build ourselves on failures. They are our learning blocks. Why should we be afraid of them?' said Rahul with complete authority.

'For most part of my journey, I have dreamt of this target. I promised guru ji that I will participate with his permission only. Now his reluctance is making me nervous'.

Rahul responded instantly, 'Don't be! Fear is just the figment of our imagination. Our self-doubts feed it and make it strong. Your fear is like that of a child who is scared of dark. He is afraid of what might come out of it. The future too is like a blind alley; we do not know what lies ahead in it. If we choose to stay where we are, we will end up losing the opportunity to change our lives. Have confidence in your abilities, it will take you through'.

Nitin looked up in the sky and said, 'Ok. I guess, I should try'.

Before reaching home, Rahul told Nitin that he will be gone for two days for finance company's work and he should try to come home early as Arjun was still unwell.

It was a very hot and humid night and Nitin was finding it hard to lie on the bed. Nitin picked up his mobile phone and saw notification on his Facebook app. Upon opening it, he saw that Mehak had accepted his friend request. He kept scrolling through her pictures and profile, until at about 1 o'clock at night, he saw that she came online on the messenger. Though he was unable to sleep, but his eyes were getting heavier. Unable to think clearly, he typed, 'Hi'.

After sending the message he felt, what a fool he had made of himself in sending the message to her at this time. He was holding his forehead in dismay when the phone buzzed. It was the reply, 'Hi'.

Nitin did not know what to say next. However, he was saved of the trouble as she wrote, 'Aren't you the guy, whom everyone calls the 'physics genius?'

Nitin felt that though for him it was a complete crush on her, but for her it was probably curiosity, but at that moment all that mattered to him was that she was talking to him. Nitin responded, 'Yes. I work in the photostat shop outside your college and I am the same guy'. He continued, 'Tell me how did you find out that it was me when I do not even have profile pic'.

Mehak dropped a smiley and typed- 'Sixth sense of girls'. Again, a smiley.

There was pause from both the sides.

Mehak- 'It was simple. Your friend list consists of what three, five or six persons? Most of them are the guys working around the college'.

Nitin- 'Oh! Then I should be grateful to these guys'.

Mehak- 'Why so melodramatic? Is it a big thing?'

Nitin felt as if his feelings were about to be discovered. He said- 'No, no. It was just a figure of speech'.

Mehak- 'Tell me, how did you solve the test series and your English is not too bad for the kind of work you do. What's your story mate?'

Nitin- 'What story? It's just that I always like physics and can't a paltry worker have a good command over any foreign language?'

Mehak- 'Aah... nice attitude too'.

Nitin dropped a smiley.

Mehak- 'So you are one of the wizards who can solve the

tough numericals of books of authors like D.C. Verma, Resnick -Halliday and Irodov without going to school just because you like physics?'

Nitin- 'Who said, I didn't go to school?'

Mehak- 'Leave it. I have heard that D.C.Verma sir had asked you to join his coaching centre, but you refused?'

Nitin- 'From where do you guys get such news. It seems that the college is less interested in studies than in my affairs'.

Mehak- 'Don't be on cloud nine, OK. It is just that few of my classmates were talking about it'.

Nitin felt that she had got offended by his statement. Now, he had to cover that up too.

Nitin- 'By the way, its half truth. He did ask me to join him, but I did not refuse'.

Mehak- 'So are you joining him? That will be nice... then you won't have to lean over the counter to see me'. She dropped a winking smiley.

Smile escaped from Nitin's lips.

Nitin too dropped a smiley and typed- 'I didn't say, I am joining. Honestly I don't know if I will! Are you also student of Verma sir?'

Mehak- 'Yes. Rocket scientist. Anyway, so you will still have to lean over the counter some more then'.

Nitin dropped three smilies. Now it was his turn to shower some praise on her. 'You are so different while chatting. Outside the college, it seems that you would hardly be speaking to anyone?'

Mehak- 'Surprise... surprise! What do you expect me to do outside college? Come and talk to you? The whole college would be talking rot then'.

Nitin- 'I didn't mean that. It is really nice of you to have replied today'.

Mehak- 'No big gain champ. It's ok. Ok, I have got to go now, I have tuition class in the morning as well'.

Nitin- 'All right. Goodnight... can we chat some other time too'.

Mehak-'Why?'

Nitin was pixelated by the query. He decided it's better to give an honest answer to such a question. 'It felt good chatting with you'.

Mehak- 'Ooh... Listen up boy. Don't be a Casanova.... It was just a chat ok?'

Nitin- 'Calm down Mehak ji'. He wrote in sarcastic manner. 'I am no Casanova. It's ok, if you don't want to chat. No problem'.

Mehak- 'Ok, ok! But then you will have to clear some of my physics related queries as well'.

Nitin smiled from ear to ear and instantly wrote. 'Sure.... I will be at your service madam...', and dropped a smiley.

Mehak- 'GN catcha'.

Nitin-'Good night'.

Then Mehak went offline. Nitin dropped his phone on his chest and smiled and smiled. I felt like jumping up and down and running down stairs and wake up Rahul bhaiya for sharing what had just happened. The clock was already striking two and better sense prevailed and he decided not to go downstairs. He decided to wake up early and catch Rahul bhaiya before he leaves early in the morning. He could not wait for sharing this news with him.

Discomfiture is the scourge for a sound sleep, whereas, bliss is its chum. The late night's gabfest had dispelled the day's anxiety. He finally fell into sleep's lap whilst thinking about her.

□

Chapter - 15

The next morning, Nitin could not get up on time, despite repeated snoozing of his alarm. When he woke up, it was already 6:45 a.m. He quickly rushed downstairs to find if Rahul was still at home, but Poonam Aunty told him that he had left for Delhi early in the morning. Nitin regretted having overslept. He went to Arjun's room who was also asleep. Nitin was getting late for his music class, so he quickly got ready and left in a hurry.

The day passed fairly quickly and there was air of positivity around Nitin. Shankar Lal too asked him about the reason of his new found happiness. Nitin warded of the query by saying that very soon, he will see him on TV as he was going to participate in a reality show. Shankar Lal giggled and asked him to concentrate on the work.

In the evening, Nitin took permission from Shankar Lal to leave a little early with the promise to complete his work of typing at home. He had to go for practice session to guruji's class and then had to be at home early as well. At night Nitin hardly got any opportunity to talk to Arjun alone as Sonia remained seated in the room. She was completing her homework. However, Nitin was determined to share his good news with his friend and made the most of a small window of opportunity which came about for 2/3 minutes when Sonia went to kitchen for fetching a cup of tea for both of them.

Arjun's spirits also got raised as it was really unexpected news. Both of them giggled and were talking in hush-hush voice, when Sonia came in.

After dinner, Nitin did not wait around and straight away marched towards his room. He opened his laptop for work, but before that he opened up his Facebook and Messenger. He could hardly concentrate on his work as he was predominantly focused on the red dot in the messenger in front of Mehak's name. His zestfulness was gradually fading away with time and he was about to give up and given to sleep, when the dot turned green at 1:05 a.m.

Nitin started the chat and the reply also came at once. Again, Nitin slept at the same time and he was at cloud nine. Everything he wanted was falling in place.

The next day in the afternoon, Nitin was working at full pace to complete his work as he had to leave early again. In the heat of work, he did not notice several missed calls from Arjun's phone number. Till date he had never received any call from any one of them at that time. He had unpropitious feeling that something ominous had happened. He tried calling back, but the number was not connecting. In those tense moments, his thoughts wondered if Arjun was alright.

Finally, Arjun's phone rang and after 4/5 rings his mother picked up the phone. Instead of listening to anything, she kept crying. Nitin kept asking, 'Aunty what has happened? Why are you crying? Is Arjun alright?' After sometime, she tried to answer but the noise from behind made her inaudible. Nitin could make out that they were travelling in an auto rickshaw. After few seconds, finally he heard Sonia's voice. He again repeated, 'What has happened?'

She spoke loudly in the phone, 'Police had called up. They have arrested Rahul bhaiya. Now we are going to Police

Station- Cantonment. You too come there'. Then she hanged up.

Nitin could not believe his ears that Rahul had been arrested by police. Seeing him in in such condition Shankar Lal asked him about what had happened? Nitin told him the news. He suddenly blurted, 'I knew that scoundrel will do something like this'. Nitin gave him a stern look and Shankar Lal fell silent.

Shankar Lal did not allow Nitin to go alone to the police station. He also took Rahul's employer with them. When they reached police station, Sonia and her mother were standing outside. Nitin quickly went towards them and asked the reason as to why police had arrested him. Poonam Aunty told them that police was not telling them anything and were also not allowing them to meet him. She was wailing and Sonia was trying her best to calm her down.

In the meanwhile, Shankar Lal and Rahul's employer went inside the building and returned after 10/15 minutes. Everyone gathered around them as they were eagerly waiting for some news about Rahul. However, they said that the SHO wasn't telling anything except for the fact that it was a very serious matter and they were still interrogating him.

Hearing this Poonam Aunty again started screaming that her young son was being framed. She was uncontrollable and Nitin as well as Sonia were unable to pacify her. After all, she had already undergone so much of pain and agony over the last two years that news of Rahul's arrest had broken her down completely.

The bystanders were looking sympathetically at the wailing Poonam Aunty, whereas, the police officials were moving around without even registering her presence. It was a routine affair for them to listen to such wails and rants of relatives of suspects and accused persons. The repeated hearing of outcries of others can easily dry up the juice of compassion from the kindest of hearts.

All of them were made to sit outside for two hours. Everyone except Nitin, Sonia and Poonam Aunty had left when the police officials called them inside. Nitin was too scared of going inside the police station due to the fear of himself getting caught. However, he could not suffer the burden of leaving Rahul's mother and little sister alone in such condition. So, he went inside with them.

The SHO told them that they had caught Rahul red handed while transporting hawala money, but he was not cooperating in the investigation. He called Rahul inside the room and asked him to look at his poor mother and little sister and told him to disclose the identity of persons to whom the money belongs so that they could help him too. Hearing this Rahul's mother cried and shouted and banged her fists on Rahul's chest in desperation. She became so hysterical that the SHO had to called female police official, who took her out of the room.

Seeing Rahul in shackles, Sonia too couldn't hold herself back and started crying. She repeatedly asked Rahul to tell the police whatever they wanted to know. Rahul too was shedding silent tears, but he did not speak anything. Finding him unmoved Sonia went on her knees and folded her hands before her elder brother and with tears flowing from our eyes she pleaded before him to tell the names of real culprits. She said, 'Bhaiya, please do as they tell and come back home or mummy will die crying'.

Amidst all this drama which was unfolding in front of him, Nitin did not realise that his eyes were also moist with tears. He could not gather courage to say anything to Rahul.

When Rahul did not acknowledge any of their entreaties,

the SHO asked him to be taken away. Nitin lifted Sonia who was reeling on the floor and took her outside where she met her mother. Both the mother and daughter hugged each other and kept crying.

One policeman came near them and asked Nitin to take both of them to their home. He also informed that Rahul will be produced in the court on the next day. Nitin did as he was told to. They came back home very late. Arjun was lying alone in his bed and he too was extremely sad. Rahul was after all not just their brother and son, he was also the head of the family now and the care taker for all of them.

The next day Nitin along with Poonam Aunty went to District Courts. After long hours of wait, Rahul was produced in the court by police. The police officials asked the court to send Rahul to their custody for four more days as he was not cooperating and the source of huge windfall recovered from him was still unknown. The free legal aid advocate provided to Rahul mumbled something which was inaudible to most of the people present in the court. The judge sitting on the dais asked Rahul, if he wanted to say something? Rahul remained tight lipped yet again. Nitin and Poonam Aunty were standing in the corner of jam-packed courtroom and were quietly observing the proceedings which had a major impact on their lives. In a minute or two, the judge granted Rahul's custody to police for a day.

As the police officials were about to remove Rahul from the court room, Rahul himself spoke and requested the judge to permit him to meet his family members who had come. His request was allowed and a meeting of five minutes with relatives was allowed in the court.

Rahul's mother could not speak anything and kept crying. Rahul on the other hand was much more composed today and he reassured his mother that he will be free soon. Nitin quietly asked Rahul, 'Bhaiya why didn't you tell their names? You would have got scot free? Why are you protecting them?'

Rahul mumbled in Nitin's ears, 'Don't be a fool! Having caught me with money, they would have never allowed me to let go. It was just one of their tactics'.

Nitin again spoke in a stern voice, 'What difference it would have made to us?'

'A lot of difference! You don't know these people. They wouldn't have spared us'. He said in a hushed tone and then continued, 'Now listen to me very carefully. We owe a debt to this company M/S N.A.V Financial Pvt. limited. It was their money. Today you go to their office at Mall road and tell them that if they don't waive the entire loan, then I will start spilling the beans in the court tomorrow'.

The suggestion shook up Nitin from within. Suddenly his mind was flummoxed as to how he could go and cut out such a deal with crooks like them.

Rahul saw the expressions on Nitin's face and said, 'You will have to do it brother or we will never be able to come out of this debt trap. This is the only opportunity for us to get it waived from these goons'.

Then they saw the police officer coming to take Rahul away. Rahul quickly added, 'Don't forget to take clearance certificate from them and don't tell anything to mummy or anyone'. The police then took him away.

On their way back, Rahul's mother continued sobbing, cursing her fate and kept whining as to what will happen to their family now. Sitting beside her, Nitin was not able to register anything which she was saying. Rahul's words were ringing in his ears. The face of the guy on the bike kept appearing before him. His heart was pounding and he was sweating profusely. He felt like running out of the autorickshaw.

After reaching home, Nitin took the stairs and went to his

room. Lying on his bed, he was finding it difficult to breathe. He got up and gulped a glass of water.

His thoughts went back to the day he had seen Rahul in the train and how daring he had appeared to him. Then he remembered how Rahul had saved him from dogs on that night and had taken care of him as an elder brother by bringing him in his house. Rahul had always stood by him selflessly, whereas, he could not do anything for him or his family. Moreover, what Rahul was asking him to do was for the entire family. The same family who had never let him feel that he was not one of them. He thought, if Rahul would have been in his position, what would he have done for him?

The last thought injected a strong determination in his feeble heart to stand by his friend and his family in this hour of their need. Nitin stood up and directly went towards the main gate of the house.

In the waiting hall of M/S N.A.V Financial Pvt. limited, he was greeted by the same person, who was driving the motorcycle the other day. Nitin went up to him and said, 'I want to talk to the owner of this company'.

'Aren't you the same little guy who was with Rahul the other day?' asked the big guy.

'Yes'. Answered Nitin softly.

'What brings you here?' asked the man.

'I have a message from Rahul, which I will share with your owner only'. Nitin gathered all the courage to say it.

The big guy gave Nitin a stony look. Then he stood up and went inside the room adjoining to the lobby. Nitin was sweating profusely and his heart was racing. He was trying his best to keep a calm face. After five long minutes, a bell rang and the peon went inside. He came outside and asked Nitin to go in.

Nitin entered into a big room which had a huge table and four visitors chairs in front of it. There were sofa sets on both sides of the table. A big Sikh gentleman with sharp features, dressed in a brown coat with white shirt below it and red cravat was seated on it. The big guy was standing by the side of the table although there was ample sitting space in the room.

The entire ambience of the room was further accentuating Nitin's restlessness. Without asking Nitin to sit, the man sitting on the chair said, 'Tell me, what message you want to give?' The man had a hoarse voice.

Nitin cleared his throat and spoke in trembling voice. 'He wants you to waive off the loan'.

'Hmmm', said the man on the chair. 'Did anyone see you coming to this place?'

'No, I don't think so'. Said Nitin.

'Are you coming straight from court or police station?' He shot another question.

'No, I went to house first'. Nitin replied.

'Ok'. He paused and started fidgeting with the paper weight kept on his table. 'Son aren't you afraid of what you are doing?' He spoke again as he leaned forward on the table. Without waiting for the response, he spoke in loud voice this time. 'You are trying to blackmail us!'

Nitin's demeanour was giving away the turmoil which he was going through. He mustered courage and said, 'Yes sir I am scared, but this is a message from Rahul which I have to deliver and if I don't go back with clearance certificate to the court tomorrow, I don't know what he will do'.

The man smiled. 'Great! You are afraid and yet you are doing it. You must be having a strong reason to do it. Do you even have any idea what we can do to you or to your friend? Now let me tell you the real story, this Rahul who is your friend or whatever, his family still owes a loan of five lac rupees to me. They hardly pay up instalments of interest and for returning the principal amount he had volunteered to do this job for which he gets Rs.25000/- per visit, which we deduct from the principal amount of loan. Due to his foolishness we have already suffered a setback of twenty- five lac rupees and you are asking me to waive the loan? If he cooperates then we can arrange a good lawyer for him'.

Nitin's instructions were clear. He gave a plain look to the man and said. 'True... but somehow still the principal amount never reduces'.

The man on the chair gave Nitin a very hard look. Nitin's last sentence gave clear indication to him that no matter what, Nitin was not going to get scared and he did not have any control over Rahul at that time. Then he turned towards the man standing beside and said, 'Clear the loan from accounts books, but don't waive it off overnight. Tell the accountant to do it'.

Nitin and the big guy turned around to leave the room. The owner of the company spoke again and as they turned, he addressed to his man to issue a personal loan of Rs.5000/- in Nitin's name. Nitin was surprised and after coming outside, he said he didn't want a loan. The big guy scoffed and said, 'Nobody is giving you a dime'. It is just to cover up, just in case you were being followed here. Nitin was out of the office in fifteen minutes with the clearance certificate in his pocket.

The cocktail of strong emotions and adrenaline rush can be so delirious to human mind that it obliterates the fine line which divides stupidity from crime. After coming out of the building, Nitin felt his legs trembling. It was then that he realized the depth of his puerility and its possible ramifications. There was hardly any difference between what Rahul had done and what he just did. Except for the fact that he had gotten away with it!

□

Chapter - 16

The mood at home continued to remain somber. It seemed as if hopelessness had casted a web around everyone. Rahul had been sent to jail and his application for bail filed by the advocate provided free of cost by government had also been rejected.

At the advice of Rahul's employer, Nitin and Rahul's mother went for appointment with the famous lawyer of the city Mr. D.S.Sidhu. His office was situated in a posh locality of Green Avenue. He had a huge bungalow and both of them were awestruck by the swanky office which had books kept in posh wall-to-wall shelves.

Both of them met Mr. D.S. Sidhu and narrated their story. He examined their documents and FIR. After reading the documents in detail he opined that they should wait for another 10/15 days as there was no chance of getting bail before that. Rahul's mother hesitantly asked about the fee that he would charge for the case. In response, he promptly told them that he thinks that it will be difficult for them to pay his fees. On her insistence, he told that he charged fee of Rs.2 lacs per case. Hearing this both of them were utterly shocked. They could never pay up such huge fees. He spoke again and said that considering their condition, he was ready to waive half of his fee. However, Poonam Aunty's eyes swelled up and she said that she had come to him with lot of faith and expectations, but they will never be able to manage such a big amount.

Mr. Sidhu clearly told her that being a professional it was the maximum he could do as he had stopped taking pro bono cases and there were many good lawyers in the city whom they could engage. However, upon Poonam Aunty's repeated requests, he agreed to accept Rs.50, 000/- as advance and the remaining fee as and when Rahul gets released on bail.

While going back, Poonam Aunty kept crying. At home, while having dinner Nitin tried to console her by saying that she shouldn't worry as they will find a way. She looked at both her children and said with tears in her eyes that now they will have to sell their house because she didn't have any jewelry left.

Nitin desperately wanted to save his friend from the deep hole he had landed into and for that good lawyer was necessary. In his room, he counted his savings. He had saved about Rs.15000/-. He thought about borrowing some amount from Shankar Lal and remaining from Rahul's employer.

The next morning, he went to Rahul's employer first and asked for some advance, however, he flatly refused to give any amount and said that he had given the job to Rahul due to his father's goodwill, but now he can't even keep Rahul on job as and when he comes out. The hostility in his voice deflated Nitin's spirit and he couldn't think of asking help of Rs.35, 000/- from Shankar Lal.

Finding no other option Nitin decided to go to DC Verma's coaching institute in the evening. After the day's work as he reached the coaching centre, D.C.Verma was about to leave. Nitin told him of his intention to work with him. Verma sir happily greeted him and took him to his office inside the centre. Sitting in his office, he informed Nitin that initially he will pay salary of Rs.18000/- p.m, but it will be raised subsequently.

Nitin told him that he wanted two month's salary in advance as he was in urgent need of money. Verma sir initially appeared skeptical, but he agreed on the condition that Nitin will have to sign a bond to which Nitin also readily agreed.

D.C.Verma took out the agreement from the drawer of his table and lo! The bond was executed. He gave advance of Rs.36000/- to Nitin and asked him to join from the next day. Nitin requested for a day's time to complete the work from old job and even offered to return the money till he joined the job, but D.C. Verma was impressed by his honesty as well as naivety and he asked him to keep the money.

When Nitin reached home, everyone was sitting around Arjun. Nitin took out the packet of money and placed it before Rahul's mother. Then he explained that he had joined a new job in a coaching centre. He asked Aunty to pay the fees and engage Mr. Sidhu as Rahul's lawyer.

There was complete silence in the room. Poonam Aunty held Nitin's face and gave blessings to him. When Nitin looked towards Arjun, he curled his lips, as if to ask why did he do it? With sadness written over his face Nitin winked back to say that there was no other option.

The next morning as Nitin was taking Arjun upstairs for his 'Tulsi Pooja', he saw that Sonia was still not ready for school. He asked Arjun, if she was fine. Arjun told him that she had decided to drop from school. The news came as a big surprise for Nitin. 'But why? She is just 13 years old', asked Nitin.

Arjun- 'I have been talking to her since yesterday, but she is insisting that she will start working in a boutique'.

Nitin was getting irritated. 'How will she work and in fact how can she work? What did Aunty tell her?'

Arjun- 'Mummy isn't saying anything. All she says is that she herself will work in people's houses'.

Hearing all this shattered Nitin from within. He was dejected that all this had happened and nobody had even thought of discussing it with him. After all, now he believed that he had the moral authority to be part of the house in some way, if not the way Rahul was.

Nitin- 'Nobody even thought of discussing anything with me?'

Arjun- 'What can I say friend? You have already done so much for us'.

Nitin spoke in terse voice. 'Please keep quiet. What have I done? You guys make me feel as if I am a part of your family and then you don't let me do anything'. His body became stiff and he said, 'I won't let this happen!'

Nitin and Arjun came down stairs. Arjun sat on a chair in the courtyard and Nitin went to the kitchen. Both Poonam Aunty and Sonia were present there. He spoke in a brittle voice. 'Aunty ji both of you have made big decisions and I don't even know of it? Am I not like your son?' Then he looked at Sonia and said, 'Am I nothing to you little sister? Do you know how much pain your decision has caused me? Both of you had never let me feel even for a moment that I was an outsider and now I am learning that Aunty will mop floors of people's houses and you Sonia would leave the school. Truly, it has shattered me from inside'.

Poonam Aunty interjected. 'No my son. It's not like that. You are already contributing so much; you must be having your own personal responsibilities. How can we burden you further?'

Nitin spoke with spunk. 'This is my only family. Only you guys are my family. I have no other responsibility except taking care of all of you, especially till Rahul bhaiya returns and Arjun gets alright'.

Poonam Aunty shook her head in anguish. Then she looked for support towards Arjun, but he turned his gaze downwards. Then as she was about to speak, Sonia interjected. 'Its ok mummy we can't take any more help from anyone'.

Nitin spoke instantaneously. 'Anyone? Am I not like your brother?'

Sonia spoke with aplomb and maturity of an adult. She said, 'It's true bhaiya. You are like my brother, but there is a difference between a brother and brother like person. Please don't mind. I respect you like my brothers, but I respect my father's principles more'.

Very quickly Nitin understood the reason behind Sonia's decision and adamancy. He tried to pacify her and said. 'It's ok, but it is just a matter of few months. Rahul bhaiya will come back and Arjun will also be fine, then they can return the money to me. Will it be fine?'

Sonia- 'It's not about you. It's about us. Never in our life, have we ever been dependent on anyone and the nature of work we do, does not matter anymore. We are already the talk of the town. The entire locality is already talking about us. We people survive in such ecosystems where perceptions turn into believes very quickly. The world is full of people like us, doing menial works. It doesn't matter to anyone'.

Arjun tried to convince her. 'But Sonia your studies are important and it's just the matter of time'. Before he could complete his sentence, Sonia spoke again. 'Papa wanted bhaiya to be a chartered accountant. You know it well that amongst all of us he was the best student. Bhaiya also wanted to fulfill Papa's dream, but look where he is now, rotting in the jail! How does it matter if papa's dream of making me a teacher is fulfilled or not? If it is my destiny, I will fulfill the promise I made to his burning pyre and God willing one day I will teach in the same school where he did'.

Nothing Nitin or Arjun said made any difference. Sonia remained firm on her decision. She glared at Arjun and he couldn't say another word.

Nitin had never thought that she was such a feisty character. He made another effort to convince her by saying. 'I adore your self-respect little sister. I told you yesterday only that I have joined a new job. I made a promise to Rahul bhaiya. Please let me keep it for some time at least'.

Sonia was not to be swayed so easily. She groaned and said, 'Bhaiya... Please leave us to our own devices'. She got up and went to the other room.

The last night, Nitin had kept thinking how he would face Shankar Lal. On the way to work, instead of thinking about his predicament of facing Shankar Lal, Nitin kept thinking of how such a young girl was so determined and resolute. How she was determined to sacrifice anything for her dignity and self-respect. He looked back and realized that at her age he was not even able to decide which subject he should study first and here was a girl who knew more about grace than anyone else he ever knew. It helped Nitin in settling the butterflies in his stomach once and for all. He learnt a lesson for life, 'we have to do, what we have to do. Its better if we do it with grace'.

On reaching the shop, Nitin took the keys from Shankar Lal as usual and opened the shop. He cleaned the shop while Shankar Lal did his routine Pooja by lighting incense sticks. Once everything had settled down, Nitin bowed down before Shankar Lal and touched his feet. Shankar Lal was astonished by this sudden show of respect, but the bigger surprise was still awaiting him. He lifted Nitin from his shoulders and said, 'Son respect is always in your heart' and he tapped at his chest and continued 'and not at my feet'. Your regular 'Namaste' is good enough as a mark of respect for me. You don't need to do it again.

Nitin's head hanged towards the ground and he said, 'I do not know how to thank you enough uncle for what you have always done for me. I am sorry, but I will have to leave you today'.

Shankar Lal was completely surprised. He curled his eyebrows in surprise and twisted his neck to look at the downward looking face of Nitin. 'Leave? What do you mean? Is there any problem? Let's talk about it. We will fix up everything! If you want your salary increased, I will do it'.

'No uncle. I don't have any issue here. It is just that due to changed circumstances, I have to move on. One-day D.C. Verma sir came up here, but you were not present and he offered me a job. I have much greater responsibilities now and I will have to go'. Said Nitin.

'How much salary? Tell me, I will give it to you'. Said Shankar Lal in agitated voice.

Nitin kept quiet. He knew Shankar Lal had to react and he was mentally prepared for it.

Shankar Lal's temper went out of control. 'I knew that scoundrel boy will take you down with him. He has landed himself in jail and will also pull you down with him. You youngsters will always remain naive. You will never understand people. All the time, I tried my best to protect you, but what else could be expected of you? Earlier you ran away from your house and now you are running away from here. All the love that I gave you and this is the response to it! You are choosing that boy and his family over me. You have responsibility towards them, but no duty towards me?'

Nitin was shocked by the discovery that Shankar Lal too knew that he had fled from his house. However, he could not do anything except for being all ears to him.

After taking out his frustration, Shankar Lal's anger started melting just as it had risen. His eyes were turning red and his exasperation was visible from his behavior.

'Son, if you would have told me, I would happily taken care of his family as well for you. From the day you arrived, not even once I could think of you as an employee. You are so dear to me'. Said Shankar Lal.

Nitin opened up his heart to Shankar Lal and said, 'Uncle, I wish I had a father like you. You did everything you could for me. You have given to me something, which I always longed for- you are like a father figure to me. Believe me it has been the hardest decision of my life'. Nitin was also on the verge of breaking down, but he gathered himself up in a moment and said, 'I know I can always turn up to you. It is hurting me, but I have to go. That family is part of me and I cannot run away from this responsibility. I knew it too well that you will give away anything that I would have asked for, but I couldn't put any additional burden on you. You can take up my burden, but I cannot load the burden of my choice and decisions on you'.

After long silence, Shankar Lal spoke. 'Still it's good for you. In the coaching centre, you will be able to stay in touch with the studies. These coaching centre people are real bloodsuckers. They will hardly give you any time to study for yourself, but take my advice and do study for yourself as well. Whatever you were doing earlier, now do it with double the strength and make your life meaningful'.

The thought of staying in touch with studies had not crossed Nitin's mind earlier. He did not even plan to study because his target was clear, to become Indian idol. However, in that moment he nodded as he did not want to get into any sort of argument with Shankar Lal while he was taking his leave. Shankar Lal bid him adieu by hugging him and finally told him to stay in touch.

That night while lying on his bed, Shankar Lal softly mumbled to his wife, 'The boy left today!'

His wife Rajni was surprised. She asked him, 'Why? What happened for prompting such a sudden decision?'

Shankar Lal told her everything. Then she said, 'We can't change much things in life. Maybe it was his destiny. Maybe this was meant to last this long only, but you did everything in your means to help him and don't worry about the business. Soon you will find someone else'.

'It was different with this boy. More than anything I feel the pangs of losing a child'. Said Shankar Lal.

'Don't worry'. She said smiling and placed her hand on his chest. 'We never lose someone who is really close to us. I am sure you will find a way to stay in touch with him. Now rest, tomorrow you have to do the entire work by yourself'.

On the other side, Nitin was experiencing a feeling, which he was unable to decipher. Lying on his bed he felt like crying but couldn't. Engulfed in the grief of losing someone and the anxiousness of the undefined future, Nitin succumbed to sleep.

When the outer faculties of our mind betray us, then our inner consciousness awakens us through our dreams. That night he dreamt about the night when he had shut the window of the moving train to his father.

□

Chapter - 17

The next morning brought a new day for everyone and for Nitin it opened a new chapter in his life. The work started an hour earlier than his previous job. He could hardly attend half a class at the music academy. Guruji was kind enough to ask him to come for extra practice sessions on Sundays, which he personally supervised.

The dates for competitive exams were fast approaching and Nitin had been given the task of setting the routine practice tests, checking the answers and taking additional clarificatory classes. The new job meant spending extra hours for preparing for the topics which were to be addressed. Nitin sat in his 5 X 5 feet room for hours, even after when everyone else had left. The long days at work were followed by nights of preparation for taking up classes the next day. Amidst the hustle and bustle of new life he still missed his old run-of-the-mill job and all the love and laughter that accompanied it.

After about a month, Shankar Lal came to meet him on the premise that the work of computer printing was suffering badly and asked Nitin, if he could chip in. Nitin smilingly accepted the assignment. No matter how busy he was, he could not refuse Shankar Lal's call for help.

At nights, Nitin found refuge in scanning Mehak's Facebook profile. He wasn't chatting with her anymore.

Earlier she had dropped number of messages on his messenger account, however, Nitin missed those messages due to twists and turns his life was taking. Now having joined a job of teacher in the same coaching centre as faculty he had created an embargo upon himself not to chat with her.

One night, when Nitin was going through her profile, there was a ping from her side.

Mehak- 'Hi... what's up? I know you are online so better respond now'.

Nitin paused for a moment and she wrote again. 'What's the matter with you? Why are you acting so pricy?'

Nitin felt compelled to respond. 'No. I am sorry, I couldn't respond to your messages earlier as I was busy somewhere else'.

Mehak- 'Anyway, welcome to the coaching centre Sir...'. And dropped a smiley.

Nitin- 'Thanks'.

Mehak- 'Why are you acting like a bore? How do you find the students of a centre? They are good na?'

Nitin- 'I am taking clarificatory classes of repeaters batch and yes some of them are very good'.

Mehak- 'Too bad, you won't get the chance to take up classes of fresh candidates. Lol! BTW where are you the whole day? I have never seen you in the centre?'

Nitin- 'Because you are not in the repeaters batch?'

Mehak- 'So funny....huh! Ok, I had sent two queries you did not answer'.

As Nitin was writing the answer to those queries, she wrote- 'Leave those queries now. I had solved them. You answer this fresh query...'.And she wrote the problem of thermodynamics.

Nitin felt frustrated as he had written half part of the solution, which he had to delete. He wrote- 'Will you be kind enough to tell me upfront, if you have already solved these querries as well or not?'

Mehak- 'Answer it quickly... the physics Maestro'.

Nitin explained her query.

Mehak- 'Hmmm.. you really know something about physics... happy to know that you are not a fluke'.

Nitin- 'I am happy to know that I have passed your test'.

Mehak- 'Talking of test, tell me why haven't you taken up the competitive exams? You are not so old to be a professor or something?'

Nitin felt like telling everything to her. While the battle of wits was going on in his mind, Mehak wrote- 'It's ok... leave it'.

She did not even give Nitin a chance to say that he was comfortable in sharing things with her and shot back.

Mehak-'Now do one thing, do fill up the forms of these exams the next year and try to follow me to IIT, where I will be studying this year'.

She dropped another smiley and wrote-'Good night. You continue to be the shy guy you are. I like such guys'.

She did not even wait for Nitin to say goodnight and went offline.

After a few days, the team of Indian Idol singing contest came to Amritsar city for initial rounds of selection. The posters were all over the city and the local media was also advertising it big time. Nitin too was fully geared up. The evening before the initial round of selection, Nitin went to the Golden Temple and sat by the side of holy '*sarovar*' for long time looking at the reflection of temple in the water.

On the day, Nitin stood in long queues of hundreds of

budding singers. Upon being called inside the room for the first round, his heart was pounding so hard that he felt that chest would explode. The technical judge understood the predicament and asked him to calm down and then give his best shot. He also clarified that he won't be able to give another chance after that.

Nitin took deep breaths and imagined that he was sitting before guruji. It eased him a bit. He again began on a shaky note, but this time he started striking proper notes and in matter of seconds all his anxiousness vanished. The clarity of his voice, the striking of notes on near perfect pitch, brought a smile to the technical judge's face. Nitin was cleared for the next round of singing before the judges of the contest, who were famous singers and musicians. Nitin came out of the room ecstatic; he was another step closer to his dream.

He sat amongst the few selected candidates. All of them were charged up and extremely enthusiastic for the next round. The confidence exuded by other candidates made Nitin more nervous. Some were saying that that they have been practicing since the age of 5 years, some were saying that they had travelled several places to learn different forms of classical music and there were also some who said that they had cleared this round even earlier and this time they knew what the judges wanted.

Finally the panel of judges started calling the candidates in the performance room. Some came out of the room crying, few came out happy and fewer came out jumping in the sky. The wait for his turn and the reaction of other contenders made Nitin extremely nervous. He was missing the presence of someone by his side to help him calm his nerves. He kept drinking water or tapping his feet in excitement.

Finally, Nitin was called inside. He got up from the seat, closed his eyes and remembered the face of his guruji. He felt better and his nerves eased. Nitin's eyes got dazzled with the bright focus lights on the stage. He had never been on such a stage before. Except the camera crew and the judges no other person was present in the room. Nitin took 4/5 seconds to adjust to the bright lights. His expressions made one of the judge's chuckle.

Right at the moment, the butterflies began to dance in his stomach again. He began the song he had rehearsed a zillion time. The initial notes went haywire. He recovered well in the middle and end, but it was not a flawless performance. The judges did not seem impressed. Nitin's heart was beating at the speed of a bullet train.

Nitin realised his mistakes and cursed himself. Two of the judges appeared very clear that Nitin was not going ahead in the next round. Luckily one of them got stuck. He asked Nitin to point out the mistakes that he had committed and then Nitin earnestly pointed out those mistakes. That made the judge even more buoyant and he insisted that Nitin should sing another song, but perfectly now.

Nitin was happy to have got another chance, but as he was about to sing another song which he had rehearsed well, the same judge said loudly, 'Don't be technical. Sing the song which is closest to your heart'.

His friend Arjun's advice rang in his ears, "We do *kirtan* for ourselves and not for others." Nitin closed his eyes and his mother's face came up before him. Nitin did not open his eyes and began singing, '*Chanda hai tu....*' Initially the judges thought how simple a song he was singing at such big stage, but soon their opinions changed. There was a deep sense of attachment and love which came out with Nitin's voice.

Nitin opened his eyes couple of seconds after completing the song.

The judges and camera crew gave a thunderous applause to Nitin and he was cleared for the next round scheduled for 4 days later in Delhi. That night Nitin realized the deep connection between emotions and art. He knew that he had still not been able to hit the perfect notes, but the deeply embedded emotions in it had made a simple song a ticket to the next round.

Nitin too came out extremely happy, but he did not have anyone to share this happiness with. He felt like shouting at the top of his lungs because he wanted to share his happiness and achievement with someone.

It was about 1'o clock at night. Nitin couldn't find any cab or other transportation. Luckily he met a person who was going to the place near his house. At times when loneliness bites, one can share his feelings even with a stranger. Talking to that stranger he realized that if he progresses in the competition then he will have to stay in Mumbai for approximately 2 to 3 months. The realization of this fact drowned Nitin in the deluge of his thoughts. Thinking about the possibility of leaving the city for such a long time sent shudders down his spine. It was obvious that for achieving his dream he had to swallow the tough pill.

It was a predicament which did not have any solution without paying heavy cost, neither of which Nitin wanted to pay. On top of it, he did not want to discuss it with the only person available at that time i.e. Arjun. He passed the remaining part of night lying awake in his bed.

The next morning, Nitin got up and quickly got ready. In about half an hour's time, he was standing in front of guruji's academy. While mumbling his prayers, guruji opened the door and was surprised to find Nitin at that time.

Guru ji continued his prayers and motioned Nitin to come inside. Nitin's face depicted his anxiousness. The dark circles around his eyes appeared even more darker. He was fidgeting with his fingers while waiting for guru ji. Guruji had never seen him so restless ever before. He too got unnerved due to the state in which Nitin was.

Guruji unrolled the mats and asked Nitin to sit. Then he poured a glass of water and asked him to have it. Nitin took a sip or two and kept the glass besides him. Instead of sitting at his regular seat, guruji also sat beside him.

'Guruji... I am in a big problem. I don't know what to do?' Spoke Nitin nervously.

Guru ji spoke comfortingly by putting his hands-on Nitin shoulders. 'Son, why are you so worried? Don't worry, just calm down and tell me'.

There was a lot of comfort in guruji's voice, but it did not have any effect on Nitin who appeared to be on the verge of nervous breakdown. He spoke, 'I cleared the preliminary rounds of Indian Idol contest'.

Nitin's words brought relief to guruji. He smiled and said, 'Well, that is a very good news. Then where is the problem? If you need any financial help, then don't worry!'

Nitin said, 'Guruji, I will have to go to Delhi and stay there for a week. If I clear that round, then as you know I will have to go to Mumbai for further rounds of the contest'.

Guruji asked quizzically. 'Then where is the problem son?'

'What will happen to Rahul bhaiya's family for these two-three months?' Said Nitin while fidgeting with his fingers.

Guruji was aware of the entire situation. Nitin had

updated him with details of Rahul being lodged in jail and all the problems that came after that as well about the change of his job. Guruji kept quiet for a while and then said, 'So, my dear son, now you can't decide, whether to follow your dream or to perform your duty'.

Nitin was in all tears now. Guruji placed his hand on Nitin's head. He understood that it was a quandary which would make the most mature of people look clueless and Nitin was just a young boy. At that moment, when Nitin was crestfallen, a strong sense of pride filled guruji's chest. Before him was a young boy who had so much conviction for the trust reposed in him.

Guruji said, 'Dear, it will be a decision which will tear your heart either way, but behold my words, no matter what you decide, God will always bless you for your decision. There can be nothing purer than the heart of a person who is thinking of sacrificing his most precious thing'.

Nitin remained silent. He expected a solution from guruji which he did not have. Guruji understood that Nitin had already made up his mind and he also knew that Nitin's decision might tear him apart.

Guruji spoke again. 'You have my blessings, go ahead to Delhi. The almighty who has brought such misery on them will also find a way to alleviate it. If you win the contest, you can bring the prize money to them. Maybe you have been selected by the will of God to help them'.

Guruji's words had temporary comforting effect on Nitin. He regained his composure and thought for a while. Then he said again, 'Guruji how will they meet the expenditure of buying Arjun's medicines when they won't even have the money to buy groceries. Arjun will not be able to survive for two months without his proper diet and medicines. His mother will have to mop the floors of people houses and clean their dirty utensils'. A lump arose in his throat. 'I will not be able to forgive myself for it. I won't be able to even sing I suppose. They have always treated me like their family. I can't leave them alone in this condition'.

Guruji tried to reassure him. 'I know, how badly you want to participate in this contest and you had left everything for achieving this goal didn't you? I am telling you it won't be easy for you, if you quit now'.

Nitin's eyes swelled up and he hugged guruji. Now he also realized that he had already made the most painful decision of his life. He was going to sacrifice his cherished dream! Guruji's eyes also got moist and he felt that his insistence was making it even more painful for Nitin. He gave blessings to Nitin and said, 'Today you have made your *guru* a thousand times prouder than you would have had done after winning the show. In this battle of love and duty you have forsaken your love for your ambition. You have a noble soul my son. In this era, when trust is yet another business, you have given away everything you earned for maintaining that trust'.

Nitin wiped his face and tears and said, 'I don't know guruji, but I guess I love them more than winning the show. I can't put them in that condition for my sake'.

Guruji squeezed Nitin's shoulders and said, 'You have made a stellar decision which no ordinary mortal could have made. You have special blessings of almighty. You will get another chance to achieve your dream and God will definitely guide you to success you deserve. Don't cry now, you should be most proud of yourself. Everyone who knows you or has ever known you will be proud of you'. Then guruji took Nitin to his personal room where both of them knelt together before 'Shri Guru Granth Sahib'.

After Nitin left, guruji remained seated in the prayer room having mixed feelings of joy and sorrow. He kept asking God, why did he put a child in such tough situation? Reading the Holy Scripture, he felt the reply came from him- For those who love, it is not a choice!

□

Chapter - 18

No one except Nitin and guruji knew that Nitin had cleared the first round of Indian idol contest. For some days the news reverberated in the city that some kids had got selected, but nobody knew that Nitin was one of them. Nitin received incessant calls and messages from the organisers of the show for few days, but when he did not revert, ultimately they stopped.

Nitin immersed himself into work. He stopped attending music classes. Now he became the first to reach the centre and would be the last to leave it. Shankar Lal kept visiting him after every ten days. Nitin kept accepting the work given by Shankar Lal without questioning, even though he had clear idea that Shankar Lal could have got that work done from some other person as well. Nitin wasn't his usual self even with him, but he liked meeting Shankar Lal.

After about one and half month from the day of contest, the results of Nitin's students started coming in and the result of the batch he had taught was the best in the city. In their interactions with media, the selected candidates started mentioning Nitin's name along with D.C.Verma sir.

For the last more than one month, Nitin had become so reclusive that he had stopped visiting Rahul in jail and had also stopped having evening conversations with Arjun. Though others found it odd, but Arjun could sense the reason of his withdrawal and did not bother Nitin. In order to keep himself busy Nitin kept taking the false refuge of excess work.

Nitin had seen several messages sent by Mehak, but he did not respond. On the day when the result of JEE was declared, she messaged him her rank and wrote how happy she was. However, Nitin still did not reply.

Two days later, in the afternoon Nitin was sitting in his room in the institute and there was a knock on the door. As he opened it, he saw Mehak standing outside. This was the first time he had seen her from so up close. She looked even prettier. She brought him out of the daze by saying, 'Hello sir.... Can I come in?'

Nitin nodded and picked the books from the visitor's chairs.

Mehak said, 'I have brought you sweets'. And she kept the box of sweets on his table. 'You read my messages, but did not even congratulate me'. Her smile vanished as she spoke.

Nitin – 'Congratulations. You will get a good college and good stream'. Mehak- 'You could have answered my message'.

Nitin got very uncomfortable as he was in his office.

Mehak spoke again. 'Please stop all this looking around. If you are so uncomfortable, I will leave'.

Nitin felt jittery and said, 'No... Please...I mean, I am sorry if you felt bad. I didn't mean to'.

Mehak spoke in low but angry voice. 'You are one strange person. One day you are so sweet and the next day a weirdo in you wakes up and you go missing for days'.

Nitin tried to speak, but was interjected again. 'Please don't make excuses. You had read my messages for sure. You know, why I have come here? Because I thought you were a good person and you deserved my thanks for helping me out. So, thank you!'She got up and left. Nitin stood up from his chair, but did not stop her.

In the evening, Shankar Lal again dropped by. He was dressed in black trouser and new light green shirt. It was the first thing that Nitin noticed and also gave compliments to Shankar Lal for it. Shankar Lal told him that it was his 15th wedding anniversary and he had come to take him to his house for feast. Nitin hesitated and tried to avoid by saying, that he has some urgent work. However, Shankar Lal was not in the mood to listen. Nitin took the box of sweets kept on the table with him.

At his home, Shankar Lal introduced Nitin to his family. Nitin wished Shankar Lal's wife and felt sorry that he did not bring anything special. They all had good time together and finally Nitin bid adieu to them late at night.

After Nitin had gone, Rajni and Shankar Lal were putting away dishes and Rajni asked Shankar Lal, if Nitin was always so quiet. Shankar Lal stepped aside and said, 'He was very lively, but for the last two / three visits, I am finding him very gloomy. Something is wrong with him which he does not tell. I had brought him here today to lift his spirits. Rajni held Shankar Lal from his arm and said, 'You love him so much. You should try to be more open with him. I am sure, he will tell you everything. Shankar Lal nodded and decided to ask Nitin clearly the next time'.

On the other hand that night while going to sleep Nitin was feeling the guilt of hurting Mehak, who had always been open and kind to him. Out of remorse, he took out the phone and messaged. 'I am sorry for having hurt you'.

Within a minute she replied, 'So finally you have realised your mistake. Ok fine'. And she dropped a smiley.

Nitin wrote- 'You are truly a character. In the morning you were so angry and now it seems that you had never been'.

Mehak- 'Huh...I am not a boring person like you that I will be stuck up. So did you eat the sweets?'

Nitin told a lie. 'Yes. Thanks'.

Mehak- 'How come you are free so early today?'

Nitin- 'I should be asking you this question'.

Mehak- 'BTW sir, if you remember my exams are over and now it's the party time. So, I have all the time at my disposal'.

Nitin – 'But I don't have whole night for chatting with you'. He too dropped smiley.

After many days Nitin was feeling better and was smiling.

Mehak- 'Really.... So, what better work do you have to do?'

This was not the answer that Nitin expected. He was speechless and didn't know what to say.

Mehak- 'Hahaha... You are really a 'bhondu'...but that's sweet. In fact that is the most enduring part about you'.

Nitin- 'Thanks.... Actually, I am not used to...'.

Mehak- 'What do you mean...that I am used to chatting and all?'

Nitin- 'No... No.... I didn't mean it at all. You know...'.

Mehak – 'Know what?'

Nitin – 'There is never a dull moment with you'.

Mehak- 'That's how I am and that's also for balancing your boring nature..'.

Nitin- 'Ok..'.

Mehak- 'Today... Papa was saying that I will get electronics stream in a good college'.

Nitin- 'Definitely. Even DCE is possible'.

Mehak- 'There are better colleges than that... what's the matter...? Do you have some infatuation about going to DCE?'

Nitin posted a smiley. During the days of his soliloquy he had grown comfortable with himself and now he did not feel the need to hide anything from anyone. Infact with Mehak he felt that he had someone with whom he wanted to share his story. He wrote. 'You know, I almost got in there'.

Mehak- 'What-almost? Dude... I always thought you would have qualified IIT or what?'

Nitin – 'Wo...ho... that's a compliment!'

Mehak- 'No seriously. Everybody thinks you would have qualified IIT'.

Nitin- 'That was never the expectation and I flunked it'.

Mehak- 'What was the expectation then?'

Nitin- 'Indian Idol'.

Mehak- 'Wow.... You are a singer too... Dude you are something! How can God be so generous to one person?'.

Nitin- 'Not generous! It's anything but opposite of it'.

Mehak- 'Cool.... Everything is fine?'

Nitin- 'Recently I had got selected from the first round of contest for going to Delhi'.

Mehak- 'But I didn't see you on TV?'

Nitin – 'Coz... I didn't go'.

Mehak- 'What???'

Nitin- 'Yes. Had a friend's family to look after. It wouldn't have been possible if I was away for 2-3 months'.

Mehak- 'Are you for real? Who does that? What age are you 40... 50??'

Nitin- 'There are hard realities of life which you won't understand now?'

Mehak – 'Whatever.... But to me you sound very confused'.

Nitin- 'Maybe you are right. That is why I was taking time off from everything'.

Mehak- 'Look dude.... You are obviously much smarter and sincere than me ... But taking time off without having clear picture in mind doesn't help. You need to take it on! Think about your career seriously and stop fooling around aimlessly.

It's time for you to to bring your life back on track. Everyone else will move on and you will be stuck up here. You are better than this!'

Nitin received the big shakedown that he needed. While unknowingly, he was trying to impress her with his maturity, she stripped him bare in his own eyes where he felt completely immature. Sometimes we get advice from such a corner which is completely unexpected. In that moment our preparedness to change determines our fate-whether we can be wise enough to accept or we allow the ego to block it! Hearing this advice from Mehak jolted Nitin and he couldn't speak anything for a while.

In the meanwhile finding no response from Nitin, Mehak thought that she had offended him and had said too much. She kept texting repeatedly, 'I am so sorry Nitin... I did not mean to offend you... '

After she had texted 6 times, Nitin responded. 'No Mehak... you are absolutely right. It is time for me to bring my life back on track'.

Mehak- 'No.... I did not mean anything bad for you. Please forgive me'.

Nitin- 'Today you have taught me a lesson that only a true friend could have done. I really needed this wakeup call!'

Mehak- 'So many guys keep running around me... But you know what made me..'.

Nitin- 'It's ok Mehak..'.

Mehak- 'No. There is a goodness in you which is visible even to the naked eye. It was obvious that there was something wrong with you, but what you told me has hurt me because I kind of care for you. You have already paid the price of your goodness and honesty. Now do something good for yourself'.

Nitin- 'You are right Mehak...'.

Mehak- 'But do it with a smile...Your smile is amazing. You promise me that next year you will come after me and take admission in my college as my junior. Lol!'

Nitin- 'I will try'.

After a short pause Nitin wrote. 'The first time I saw you, you looked fantastic and I started liking you, but now after finding out the real you, I not only I like you but respect you even more'.

Mehak- 'You are very good with words too...Hahaha'.

Nitin- 'Thanks for everything. Take care...'

Mehak- 'You too'.

Before that night, Nitin always felt that his life was working in binary form. The situations had presented the options to him where he had to take the decisions either in yes or no and these decisions were shaping his life. That night, he felt that his life had more to it. Now he had the desire to create his own situation which could shape his destiny.

□

Chapter - 19

After a couple of months Arjun regained his health. Though he continued to be on medication, but he had started doing all his chores by himself. He went back to the same place where he was working and was told that someone else had taken his place. Arjun felt that infact the real reason was somewhere between imprisonment of Rahul and his disease. He tried to find another job but couldn't succeed.

Shankar Lal had repeatedly told Nitin that he had employed someone, but on the visit to his home, Nitin learnt from Rajni that Shankar Lal was overburdened with work because he could not find any good new guy.

Nitin took Arjun to Shankar Lal's shop. Shankar Lal's face turned red on seeing Arjun. He frowned at Nitin and then asked him to come to the side. Nitin knew of Shankar Lal's hatred for Rahul. It was an arrangement which suited all and in a way he also wanted to placate Shankar Lal's vexation towards Rahul and his family. He was certain that Arjun wouldn't give any opportunity for complaining to him.

Shankar Lal was very agitated. His shoulders were drawn backwards and his hands were resting on the side of his waist as he asked Nitin, 'What is all this? You want me to bring these wretched people in, so that now they can play havoc with our lives again?'

Nitin tried to mollify his anger by saying. 'I understand

your point of view'. He was not allowed to complete his sentence. Shankar Lal spoke again while raising his left hand in the air gesticulating denial of the proposal and said, 'Take him back, I can't do it' and he moved back towards the shop.

Nitin spoke from behind. 'He has nothing in common with Rahul'. Shankar Lal stopped and turned. 'You are just a kid... Ok!'

Nitin said, 'True uncle, but believe me on this. He is the complete opposite of what Rahul is'.

Shankar Lal- 'Still... why should I keep him when there are hundreds of such people looking for a job'.

Now it was Nitin's turn to startle Shankar Lal with revelation. He said, 'Then why haven't you kept one so far?'

Shankar Lal turned slightly towards Nitin, but did not look him in the eye. While touching his throat, he spoke gingerly. 'Who told you this?'

Nitin went towards him and looked him in the eye and said, 'Uncle, I know you need a helping hand. Arjun is a good egg. You won't have any complaint from him'.

Then Nitin looked away and said, 'Moreover, I normally get busy with work and sometimes I don't feel like going back, but then I don't want them to think that I am running away from them which will make it difficult for me to help them. If you keep him, they will have regular income and I will be free'.

The thought of Nitin getting away from them sounded good to Shankar Lal even if it meant bringing one of them closer to himself.

Shankar Lal asked. 'What about his T.B.? It is highly contagious'.

Nitin turned his neck and said, 'Uncle! Do you think I would have brought him here if he was not well? He is completely free of T.B. He will continue to have medicine for about one year, but he is fine now'.

Both of them went inside the shop and Shankar Lal asked Arjun to come for work from the next day. In response, Arjun asked if he could start from that day itself. Shankar Lal looked at Nitin, who smiled.

Rahul's bail application had been dismissed twice now and it had been almost six months. Now, they had filed a petition in the High court which was due to come up in a fortnight. Everyone at home was tense as dismissal of this application meant that Rahul would have to remain in jail for another six months or so. Due to the anxiety at home, Nitin made it a point to come back every day, but hardly talked to anyone.

At work, besides the new repeaters batch, Nitin was given additional responsibility of handling online courses. Despite the additional work, Nitin made it a point to work on his mathematics and chemistry daily.

One day, after all the classes had got over, Nitin was sitting in his room and was studying chemistry. D.C. Verma came in and saw Nitin glued to chemistry. In a rude tone, he said, 'What is it?' Nitin stood up and meekly shook his head and said 'Nothing sir'. Seeing Nitin devoting time to other subjects DC Verma got an opportunity to be infuriated. He began shouting, 'Stop this nonsense!' Then he controlled his temper and took a breath and in controlled but angry manner said, 'During your official timings, you are not supposed to do anything else. Do not repeat it again'.

In the vein of his superiority of his position D.C. Verma was mocking his own insecurity as he was unable to accept the praises showered by the selected students upon Nitin along with him. Nitin was not even aware that his praise had pricked D.C.Verma so badly. He took the scolding in his stride and learnt a lesson about professionalism. After that day Nitin did not touch any other subject except physics during his office timings.

One-night Nitin went back home very late, but as he opened the door, he saw Poonam Aunty standing near staircase leading to his room. Smilingly she held Nitin's face and said, 'Son, your brother will be back home soon. The lawyer's clerk from High Court had called in the evening to tell that Rahul's bail application has been allowed and now we need to file the bonds only in the court and he will be released. I tried calling you but your phone was switched off'.

Nitin took out his phone from the pocket of his jeans and saw that the battery of his phone was dead. He had forgotten to charge his phone. He congratulated her for the good news. As he was climbing up the stairs, Poonam Aunty spoke again. 'I asked the neighbours, if they could stand surety but no one has agreed. Maybe if you can ask Shankar Lal bhai sahab'.

Nitin hesitated and told her that he will try. He thought that it will be asking too much from Shankar Lal. Then he pondered about asking guruji, but he had not gone to his class for last three months and had also not picked up his phone call. Even otherwise, asking a saintly person to stand surety did not seem right.

Lying on his bed Shankar Lal's words started reverberating in his head. Perhaps he was putting himself under too much of uncalled for pressure. Then as he shrugged off the thought, it occurred to him that Poonam Aunty could also stand surety. The mortgage on the house had been cleared. Though he wanted to handover the clearance certificate to Rahul upon his return, but finally he thought that it was the need of the hour.

The next morning after getting ready Nitin went down stairs and everyone i.e. Poonam Aunty, Arjun and Sonia were sitting in the room. He placed the clearance certificate before Aunty and said you can be his surety. She picked up the paper and was shocked. She was unable to speak. All of them read the certificate turn-by-turn and were shell-shocked. Nitin knew that all of them were wrong in thinking that he had got the dues cleared. He thought about telling them the truth, but now he hardly spoke unless it was necessary. He felt that he was not telling any lie to them. Even if his silence meant encouraging a false belief, he thought a falsehood which does more good than truth was acceptable to him. He had promised Rahul that he would not tell any of his family members about the real story. Quietly, he picked up his bag and left for the office.

At night, Nitin again came late but the atmosphere in the house was vibrant and lively. He straightway went to the main room and Rahul was sitting on the floor, having his dinner. His mother was sitting by his side. As he saw Nitin, he got up and hugged him tightly. In return Nitin gave him a warm pat on his back. Rahul was beaming with joy and Nitin only had a slight smile on his face. After exchanging the pleasantries Nitin took leave and went to his room. The difference in his behaviour did not go unnoticed and though Rahul felt surprised, but he chose not to show it.

Ever since his dream had come to end, Nitin had started feeling uncomfortable in Rahul's house. Being in the house constantly reminded him of the loss. He wanted to move far away and at the same time wanted an amiable exit. He told Arjun that he wasn't satisfied with the time he was able to spend for his own preparation and now he felt that he should devote more of his time to studies and focus completely on it.

The next day Nitin went to the office of administrator of the coaching centre for seeking permission from him for staying in the centre at night on some occasions. Everyone knew that Nitin generally used to be the last one to leave the centre, therefore the administrator gave him extra set of keys of one room set with attached washroom on the top floor.

Gradually Nitin's visits to Rahul's house became fewer with time. Rahul felt the disconnect and he tried to raise the issue with Nitin. One evening, he went to the coaching centre as Nitin had not returned home for the last one week. He asked Nitin, 'Why are you acting so differently? Is everything alright? I hope no one at home has said anything to you?'

In a completely calm voice, Nitin said, 'No bhaiya not at all. It is just that work is too much now a days and I wasn't getting time for my preparation, so I stay back for studying'.

Rahul-'Now, you don't go for your music classes?'

Nitin grimaced and said. 'Don't feel like going there anymore'.

Rahul-'You can study at home as well'.

Nitin knew that it would be hard for him to explain his feelings to Rahul, so he smiled and said, 'Don't worry bhaiya, I will come back'.

Rahul said, 'We miss you at home and everybody is worried about you. In case you have anything in mind, I believe you will tell me'.

Nitin smiled and nodded and said, 'of course bhaiya'.

Rahul observed that Nitin's expressions and his words did not match each other. Though he was dying to know what had prompted change in his behaviour, but he had no option but to resign to the fate. With a heavy heart, he left the coaching centre.

Nitin did not want to hurt Rahul or any one of them, but he did not feel connected with any of them anymore. He had tried to understand the reason of his nonchalance, but had failed. He only felt some emotions for Shankar Lal, who had not stopped coming to meet him ever since.

Now for Nitin studying and teaching physics during the day and studying maths and chemistry at night was the template of his life. His chatting sessions with Mehak had also reduced to minimal. She too had got busy in her new life and after sometime it just stopped.

Nitin was burning the midnight oil for his preparation, but it was totally different than how he had prepared earlier. Now Nitin was trying hard, but without any passion or ambition of clearing the exams. His target was to study well and not to enter in any particular college. His swotting was like meditation. He was diving deep into it without any dream or desire.

The slaughtering of the most treasured ambition ordinarily propels a person towards remorse or towards revolt, but in Nitin's case neither of these two occurred. He blamed himself for his decisions. He had himself stifled his cherished dream, but the pain finds a way of expressing itself. Nitin completely withdrew himself from everything and everyone.

Initially secluded in his room away from everything, Nitin often thought how cruel life was, but with experience he had also earned a different perspective. He realized that though certain losses were inevitable, but realized that some could have been avoided with investment of bit of patience and compassion. Many times, he pondered over his decision of quitting on his ambition, but everytime he thought that given the situation again, he would have done the same thing yet again. The only thing that pricked him now was the deal he had handed over to his father. He had started feeling that come what may, he should not have done this to his father.

In this period of loneliness, his dreams and the decisions

he had made started appearing meaningless to him. The busy schedule of his studies was the only thing which kept him away from skipping into deep depression. The desire to study kept him motivated still.

Amidst the gloom of self-condemnation his heart drew light from his occasional evening visits to the Golden Temple, where he chose the same place to sit again and again-the place where he had the vision of his mother. Sitting there many a times, he wondered whether it was his exhaustion which had played tricks with his mind on that day or it was really her! Nevertheless, that seat always instilled tranquillity in him. It had a view of shining temple in front and its reflection in the water. It looked as if his mother had chosen a perfect spot for him so that even when his gaze got lowered due to sadness, it still did not deprive him of the light of God.

□

Chapter - 20

As Nitin's entrance examinations approached, he completely immersed himself in the preparation. He had become an insomniac. His visits to Rahul's home and even to the Golden Temple had stopped completely. Shankar Lal had started visiting him even more. Nitin's condition had made him very anxious. He was worried that Nitin may suffer mental breakdown before the exams. His entreaties to take him home were always rebuffed. So now instead of bringing computer printing work, he used to bring him home cooked '*Pinnies*' and '*laddoos*'.

From one of the visits of Shankar Lal, Nitin came to know that Arjun had left for Mathura to be a lifelong devotee and his mother was running between the two cities with the hope that he will come back. In his heart, Nitin knew that the caged bird had flown and was not going to be fettered again.

Finally, Nitin's exams got over and his workload also got reduced. In a fortnight's period, the results too came and many of his students got selected in various IIT's. He himself scored the record-breaking marks in physics, but overall, he missed the mark for admission in IIT's nearly. He had the next best option to join either; 'BITS Pilani' or 'NIT Jalandhar' or 'Delhi College of Engineering'.

After few days the felicitation of selected candidates began in the coaching centre. Along with other selected candidates,

Nitin was also invited to the stage. In the beginning of his speech, D.C. Verma sir hailed Nitin as the source of inspiration for all the students as his selection had set a shining example that hard work and determination can definitely lead you to success. He also added that he never had a doubt that Nitin will be successful in the examinations and today he was so proud of him.

Hearing DC Verma speak, Nitin hanged his head and smiled. He doubted if earlier Verma sir was even aware that Nitin had taken up the exams and here he was- the same person, who had scolded him badly for studying other subjects, saying that he was proud of him.

Standing on the stage, he looked at the faces of newly joined candidates whose eyes were glued to Verma sir and all of them were believing him to be a messiah born only to take them to their destination. He realized that projections were nothing but masks of hypocrisy and inspiration was also a business commodity for such people.

Standing there Nitin felt suffocated and he did not want to waste any more time on a swindler for whom he had no respect left in his heart. He got off the stage and moved out.

Nitin's selection meant that his days in the city were over. Before his departure, Nitin spent a night at Shankar Lal's place with his family. Shankar Lal and Nitin had a unique bond between them, which instead of wilting had blossomed with the searing heat of every crisis.

Nitin also went to see guruji. He walked through the streets from where he went bustling every morning for music classes and in which he had enjoyed the evening strolls with his friends. Nitin entered in the academy and went to the class where small children were reciting '*Gurbani*'. It brought back the memories of the day when he had walked into the academy for the first time. Nitin sat there quietly till the class got over. He wanted to secure all his fond memories.

After the class, Nitin touched guru ji's feet and told him about his selection. It made guruji extremely happy and a big smile beamed on his face. After all Nitin was his most loved disciple and the news had set to rest his worries for him because his life was back on track. He again took Nitin to his personal prayer room and read prayers for his bright future. On the door of academy, as Nitin folded his hands in reverence, guruji said to him, 'If possible, go to your parents. Their dreams too would have been shattered by you running away'. Nitin looked at guruji and then quickly turned away without saying anything.

Nitin could not have left without saying goodbye to Rahul and his family. Sonia opened the door to Nitin. As they entered the living room, Rahul got up and left the house. Perhaps he knew the purpose of Nitin's visit. Sonia apologized for his brother's conduct. As expected, Poonam Aunty was in a distraught condition. Her eyes were going back to Arjun's photo time and again. In his heart Nitin was prepared much earlier that Arjun was going to leave someday, but he tried to console her and said, 'Aunty, he had already chosen his path. It was inevitable, if not now then on some other day, but he would have left anyway'.

Poonam Aunty looked towards Sonia and said, 'All of you say the same thing, but you are not parents. How would you understand my pain? We parents raise you guys, so that you may run away just like that?'

Her words pierced Nitin from within. Although her angst was directed towards Arjun, but he felt as if his father was accusing him.

In the meanwhile, both Poonam Aunty and Nitin could not

sense the anger and frustration building within Sonia. Finally, she bursted and shouted. 'You are always crying about him mother. What could he had done otherwise? Ever since I saw him with the girl next door in such a condition...'.She paused and then grunted.... 'He was always itching to run away. For three years, he was just trying to find an excuse to get away because he could not come to grip with the fact that I had seen him. Finally, he did run away. Such an escapist!'

Both Nitin and Poonam Aunty were shocked to silence and Sonia ran out of the room. Quietly they sat in the room for few more minutes and then Nitin stood up and left. Nitin had thought of finally leaving that house with memories, but instead he left it with many thoughts in his head.

After Sonia's last-minute disclosure, instead of thinking about Arjun, Nitin started thinking about himself. He too had spoken so badly to his father just before his departure and had gone on to use foul language. Every time, he had thought about the way his father had treated him, his thoughts had gone close to his own action, but he always closed his mind to it. Walking on the narrow streets of Amritsar, he realized that he was no different from Arjun. He felt as if his decision to run away was not because of any external influence of Govind uncle and may be that was just a false pretext he had created for himself. Maybe he wanted to run away from his father because he knew that his own action was unpardonable. Maybe his guilt always prevented him from looking into his mistake because he too lacked courage to face and admit what he had done! Maybe he himself could not come to terms with the fact that he could use such foul language with his own father.

Shankar Lal alone was there to see off Nitin at the railway station. He too stood waiting till the train had left the railway station. On this occasion, teary eyed Nitin did not shut the side window of his seat.

Sitting by the window side of the fast-moving train his face was flushed by the strong gusts of air. He had only one remorse-he felt the pinch of not being able to say goodbye to his friend Rahul, but what could not be cured had to be endured. He would have never associated Rahul with escaping from a situation, but who was he to judge him! The hardships inflicted by time make the strongest of rocks wither away. The brunt of time and his own emotional disconnect with Rahul had taken its toll on Rahul as well.

Nitin started thinking about the past two years. His mind was unknowingly preparing a balance sheet of profits he had gained and losses he had suffered. He felt that he was going back to the same place after two years and that too without having fulfilled the purpose for which the journey had started. Still his heart was neither filled with remorse for the last years nor did he feel emptiness. Rather he was longing for the beautiful relationships he was leaving behind. How lucky he was to have received unconditional love from everyone he had met. He felt grateful that he had forged bonds with people around him, who did not leave his side when they could have left so easily. He had respect and love for each of them who were 'gurus' to him in their own capacity. How each one of them had taught him the value of nurturing and preserving relations at every cost.

There were also people who were not so kind, but his heart and mind had came to believe that it is the situations and conditions which compel people to make bad choices, but those people aren't really bad. He was leaving the bitterness and frustration behind him and was taking the experiences and love of people with him.

In his period of two years, he tried to understand

himself better. He looked inside and felt proud of himself that even when he was under the pump, he remained true to his character if it meant making difficult choices. After all, the real test of patience and character is only when one is subjected to tough situations. After ending his own dream, he had realised that it did not matter if the purpose of his life was grand or simple. All that mattered was how dear it was to him because only then it could give him both passion and peace. What he required at that time was the synchronisation of thoughts, harmonization of feelings and channelization of energy. By clearing the entrance examination again, he had proved to himself that we are, what our thoughts make us.

□

Chapter - 21

Nitin had informed Mehak about his selection and ranking because he thought she deserved to know it. She had sounded happy, but the spark which Nitin had always felt while interacting with her was missing from both the sides.

Mehak was a student at NIT Jalandhar. Nitin had the option to join that college, but still he joined Delhi College of Engineering as he did not want go down the same road and getting stuck up again. Having saved his salary, he took admission on his own and after the allotment of hostel room he straight away went to join the music society of the college. The candidates who had opted for this college with him earlier were senior to him now, however, it did not bother Nitin.

The same night Nitin took another train. In the morning he was standing outside the front door of his house. There was a new name plate which had the name of Sushmita written on the top, Nitin in the middle and Shantanu at the bottom. He pressed the doorbell, but it did not ring; it was out of order. After 2/3 knocks the door was opened.

Time had left a distinct mark on the man who opened the door. There was a tall frame with his face fully covered in beard which had almost turned white. The grind of time had taken away his paunch and he was skinny as he never had been. The once plump face now had dark circles under the eyes, which were distinctly visible even under his spectacles.

The man kept staring at Nitin's face. Both of them did not utter a word nor any one of them moved. After a long pause the emotions swelled up within Shantanu and moistened his eyes. He flung his arms wide open. The luggage fell from Nitin's hands onto the ground and he moved into the wide stretched arms of his father. Nitin had never anticipated such reception. In fact, he was prepared to face the anger and wrath of his father, but his life had never turned out the way he had expected it to be and this was no exception again.

Nitin could feel the bones of his father in that hug. They stood still for some time and moved only when no strength was left in Shantanu's legs which had started trembling.

Sitting on the sofa, Shantanu did not let go the hug of Nitin. It was a surprise which he had not expected. Shantanu broke the silence. 'You have changed a lot'.

Nitin smiled, but remained silent. He looked around the house and it had the same look as he had seen it the last time with the only difference that the walls looked shabby and jaded and some of the artefacts had not been cleaned for some time. He got up and stood before the picture of his mother which was hanging from the wall.

Shantanu spoke again. 'I miss her very much'.

Nitin looked down on the floor and said, 'Aren't you angry with me?'

Shantanu smiled a bit and said, 'Not now. When you had left, I went into a state of panic and was extremely angry with you. Not a day passed, when I had not cursed you for leaving me like this. I tried very hard to find you. I kept running around the police stations for several months. Finally when I lost all hope of ever seeing you again, I understood that I had lost the only two people I loved in my life. Only upon understanding the loss, I was able to realize that I had never been there for you. I thought being a father, I had the right over you. How foolish I was! It was not your mistake...it was mine that you had to leave'.

Nitin- 'I am sorry for having left you when you needed me papa. You were not just harsh to us; you were also very tough upon yourself. Ma had me and I had her, but you did not have anyone. At that time when you were also trying to bear Ma's loss, I only thought about myself and left you, when I should have been there with you and on top of it...that night...' The words again just didn't come out of his mouth, but having thought about it for so long and so many times, he was determined to let it out of him. He sighed and looked up and said... 'I am very sorry for what I said that night Papa. It has haunted me ever since and I can't tell you how ashamed I am of myself for what I did that night'.

Shantanu put his arm around Nitin's shoulders and said, 'It's ok my dear son. Whatever had to happen has happened. Let bygones be by gones. Forget it'.

Shantanu looked at Nitin and smiled, but Nitin still looked away. He was still not comfortable about it and was unable to look his father right in the eye. Then he continued. 'But you were right about me. I just kept running around uselessly and missed out all the beautiful moments which I should have spent with both of you. Instead of collecting the treasure of happy memories, I was busy in accumulating few bucks in my bank which do not give me any happiness today. Son, I failed to understand the true beauty of life'.

Nitin kept looking the other way and said, 'Having travelled around, I understand your perspective. Money is also a dire necessity and it hurts you the most when you don't have it. You were trying to save few bucks for the rainy days and the whole world is control freak papa. Everyone wants control. Most parents want to control their children. I should have understood it earlier that running away from relations is not the solution to any problem'.

Shantanu- 'We all are fallible my son. We the humans are God's most imperfect creation. We all make mistakes, but we cannot undo our mistakes of past. All we can do is not to repeat it again. Now don't ever leave me again!'

Nitin smiled and with sad expression on his face said, 'I am sorry papa, but I will have to'.

His response left Shantanu pale. Nitin completed, 'I have to go to my engineering college'.

Shantanu gave a puzzled look and said, 'But, you did not join the college?'

Nitin told him that he had got selected this year again. It made Shantanu smile and he hugged Nitin again and proudly said, 'After a point of time when you were not reachable, I always thought to myself that you had gone for good for yourself. I wouldn't have let you live your life'. Tears were flowing from his eyes now. He controlled himself and asked, 'What happened to your ambition of becoming a singer? I always thought you would have had gone to Mumbai'.

Nitin laughed and said, 'You are right Papa. I left to gain fame to be a singer, but I went to Amritsar'. Then he said in a very assuring tone. 'You know I almost pulled off'. Then he giggled and said, 'Somethings are just not meant to be. Maybe your resistance was a sign of it'.

Shantanu said, 'No son, we should live our dreams and dream as big as we can. After all who knows how long we will live'.

Nitin observed that there was a tinge of sadness in his father's eyes even when he was smiling. In a concerned voice he asked, 'Is everything alright papa? You don't seem too well?'

Shantanu shrugged and said, 'No...no everything is fine. I haven't asked you, what will you have? Your mother would not spare me for not asking you to have anything'. And he laughed.

Nitin still could not accept the answer. He felt that Shantanu was hiding something from him. He spoke in a calm voice, 'Papa please tell me what is it?'

Shantanu stopped laughing and turned towards Nitin and said with a smile. 'I am so happy to see my son again in this lifetime'.

Nitin was shocked. 'What do you mean?'

Shantanu- 'I have lung cancer. My chemotherapy is going on'. Nitin's eyes became wide open and he felt as if he had been hit by a truck. He had just discovered his father and now the news that he too was going shattered Nitin and the tears again found their way to his eyes and while crying he kept murmuring, 'I am so... sorry papa. I am so... sorry'

Shantanu sat by his side and cuddled him and kept consoling him. After sometime, he said, 'It's ok ...my son, I am so happy that you have come back. Every day I used to ask your mother to send you back so that I could apologize from you, before I get united with her'.

Nitin wept uncontrollably and all he could speak was 'papa...papa...it can't be...'

Shantanu spoke again. 'See she has been so kind to me yet again'. Shantanu looked at Sushmita's photograph and kept smiling while hugging Nitin. He was extremely happy to have his son back. At the end of the road what matters the most is not what you missed, but what you have. Shantanu was not going down the road empty handed.

Nitin had already booked the return ticket after three days. He kept insisting that he will stay with Shantanu for his treatment. However, as much as Shantanu wanted to be with his son, he did not want his son to make the same mistake again and be caught in the same endless circle. Ultimately, he persuaded Nitin to go back to Delhi for his studies and asked him to come back on off days.

Once again with heavy heart, Nitin undertook another journey with the eagerness in his heart to be back soon... Earlier he had begun his journey as if life was a problem to be solved, but now he had realized that enjoying the journey as it comes, is what life is!